WHEN MYSTICAL CREATURES ATTACK!

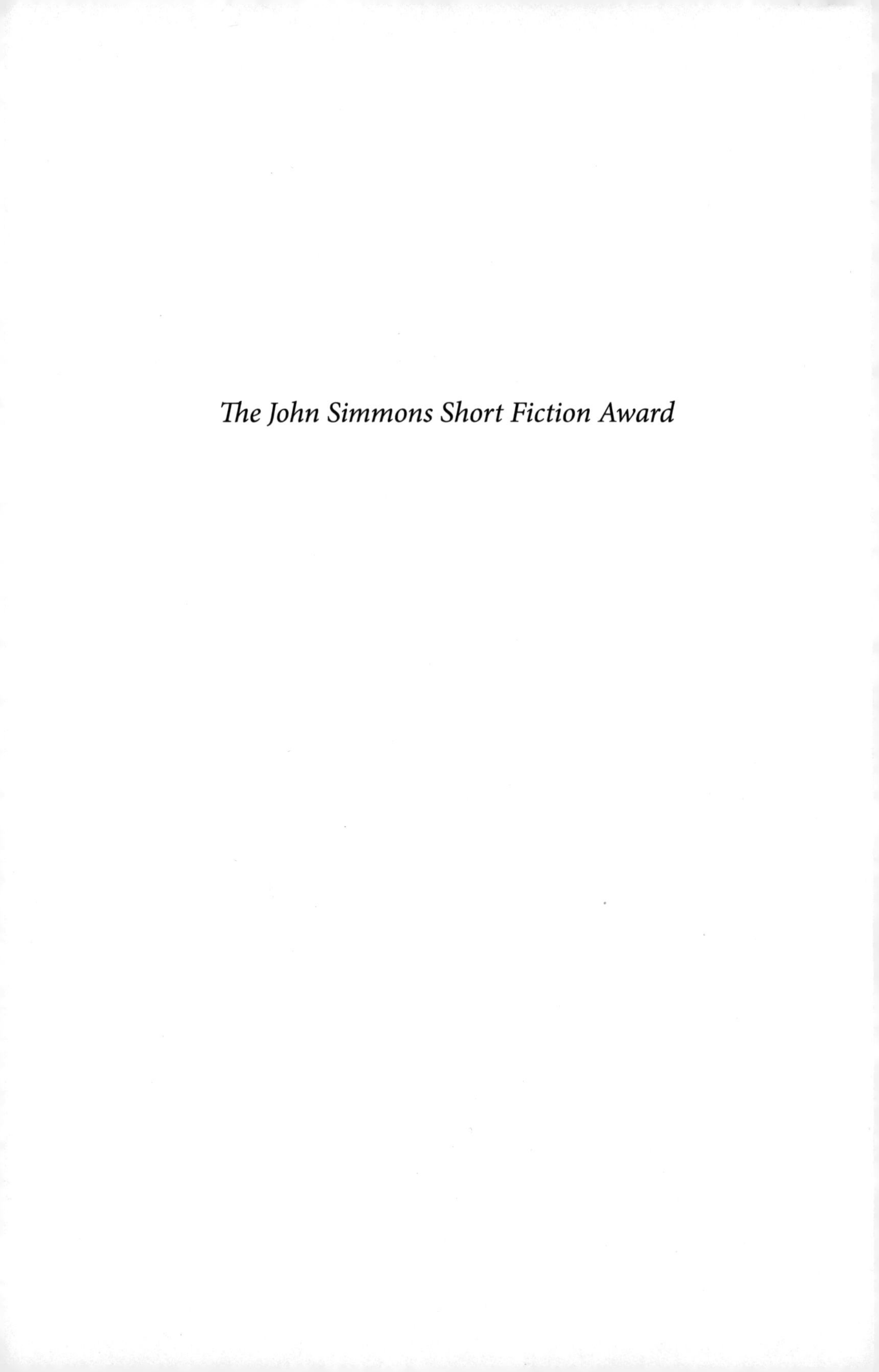

The John Simmons Short Fiction Award

Kathleen Founds

When Mystical Creatures Attack!

University of Iowa Press
Iowa City

University of Iowa Press, Iowa City 52242

www.uiowapress.org
Printed in the United States of America
Design by Ashley Muehlbauer

The University of Iowa Press is a member of Green Press Initiative and is committed to preserving natural resources.

Printed on acid-free paper

ISBN: 978-1-60938-283-4 (pbk)
ISBN: 978-1-60938-290-2 (ebk)
LCCN: 2014935648

For Summer

There is a crack in everything
That's how the light gets in.
—Leonard Cohen, "Anthem"

✲ CONTENTS ✲

᯾ ACKNOWLEDGMENTS ᯾

Thanks to my wonderful teachers: Tobias Wolff, George Saunders, Mary Gaitskill, Mary Caponegro, Tom Kealey, Adam Johnson, Michael Burkhard, Amy Hempel, Arthur Flowers, Charis Conn, Daniel Orozco, Dr. Kapolka, Dr. Raab, Professor Yearley, and Mrs. Hunt.

Mom, thank you for making the Watsonville Public Library our second home. Dad, thank you for reading *The Lord of the Rings* to all five kids. Davey, thank you for the hoppiness of Hopopotomus in our hearts. Jenny, thank you for begging for a story every night. Mikey, thank you for manic marketing. Matty, thank you for sand toads and butcher birds. Thank you, Faye, keeper of family lore. Thank you, Maura, for expanding my horizons. Thank you, Wells Tower. Without you this book would be—best case scenario—bound with string and sold out of the back of a van. University of Iowa Press, you have made a dream come true. Thank you Jim McCoy, Karen Copp, Charlotte M. Wright, Allison Means, and Christa Fraser. Thanks to Erin Gay, Stacey Petrek, and my Syracuse Workshop: you helped me survive winter. Thanks, Gideon Lewis-Kraus, for prodding me to pursue an actual writing career. Thank you Vauhini Vara: without you this book would be dust on a hard drive. Thank you, Hope House, St. Lucy's, Stanford, Santa Catalina, The Jesuit Volunteer Corps, The Inner Beauty Parlor, and Old Fashioned Days. Thank you, Texas soul mates/roommates Karen and Laura. Thank you, Nada and Harriet. Thank you, Sam. Thank you, John and Abby, for being community builders and patrons of the arts. Thank you, Summer, Heather, and Jared for enthusiastic early reads. Thank you, Daniel Blue Tyx, for your irrational exuberance. Gracias a la Iglesia Menonita Buenas Nuevas—especialmente a María Espinosa, por enseñarme que dios habla español. Gracias a la familia Hernández por su amistad y verduras. Cabrillo students, you are my inspiration. Violet, you are my heart. Dave Lazerfounds, I believe we were bears together in a past life. Thank you for your unfailing love.

Grateful acknowledgment is made to publications in which early versions of these stories appeared: *Booth Journal*: “The Un-Game”; *Epiphany*: “Recipes for Disaster”; *The MacGuffin*: “Frankye”; *Stanford Alumni Magazine*: “The Holy Innocent” (originally published under the title “One Useful Thing in My Life”); *The Sun*: “Virtue of the Month” and “When Mystical Creatures Attack!”

WHEN MYSTICAL CREATURES ATTACK!

✯ WHEN MYSTICAL ✯ CREATURES ATTACK!

1. What is your favorite mystical creature? ___________________________
2. What is the greatest sociopolitical problem of our time? ____________

____

Journaling Prompt: *Write a one-page story in which your favorite mystical creature resolves the greatest sociopolitical problem of our time.*

How the Minotaur Changed the Legal Drinking Age to 16
by Danny Ramirez

He'd be like, "Citizenry of congress, teenagers are going to drink anyway, so you need to learn to trust them, and not have the janitor break open their lockers because you think they have your diary hidden under their gym clothes," which I didn't, Ms. Freedman, so I hope they make you pay for my lock. Then the Minotaur would decree that any teacher who, in the heart of her personal journal, describes students as "feral raccoons devoid of impulse control" is maybe not cut out for education. Then the Minotaur would get hired as a Spokes-Minotaur for King Cobra. He'd be in commercials with all these big blonde Amazonian chicks, drinking forties, doing a topless carwash. In a maze.

How the Unicorn Stabbed Danny Ramirez in the Heart Seven Times, Which Is What He Deserves, for Breaking Up with Me Like That

by Andrea Shylomar

I don't believe in anything mystical, Ms. Freedman. Not even God. You made us build that diorama of Mount Olympus, and you made us paint that mural with unicorns and butcher birds and sand toads. You said it was to show that books transport us to different worlds, where there are different rules, and there's magic in everything. Well what you forgot, Ms. Freedman, is that when you shut the book, you're back in this world, and the bell is ringing, and wadded up paper is thrown at your head, and Phil Gasher is poking at your crotch with a broken pencil, and Kristi Colimote's bitchy flunkies climb into your bathroom stall and threaten you with scissors. What you need is a book that takes you out of this world permanently. Which is called a gun, I think.

How the Werewolf Solved the Problem of Hunger

by Xuang Lee Zhang

He ate everyone. Then there were no more people. Then no one was hungry. Especially not the Werewolf. He did get lonely, though. He was so fat he couldn't move, and he lay on the bank of the river wishing someone would come and sing to him. Nobody did.

How the Giant Squid Made Me Stop Being Pregnant

by Kristi Colimote

I was swimming in my bathing suit, all worried, because like I told you at lunch hour Ms. Freedman, I'm pregnant. I guess Danny Ramirez is the father, but I barely broke up with him, and already he's hooking up behind the dumpster with that fish-lipped Shylomar freak. Plus also? My mom is totally going to kick me out when she finds out.

So I was floating there, and it smelled like seaweed, and I tasted salt on my tongue, and then the giant squid grabbed me with her big pink arm. It felt all squishy around my stomach, and it pulled me under and I couldn't breathe. The squid hugged me close to her body, and told me in squid language that she would take my baby and live with it under the sea. Then she squeezed my stomach and this little fish popped out and I could tell it was going to grow up to be like this gorgeous mermaid who would drive the sailors crazy when they saw her tits all poking out of the water. The squid kind of cradled the little fish with one tentacle and then she let me go. I stuck my head out of the water and I felt my stomach and the baby was gone. I swam back to shore, all happy, because my baby was safe there in the dark water, and in my bathing suit I walked all the way over to the Planned Parenthood on 23rd Street. I was all dripping when I walked inside. The secretaries were like, "What's with this chick?" I just told them to put me on birth control, like I should have done a year ago, if I wasn't so scared of my mom finding out.

How the Sphinx Solved the Problem of Loneliness

by Cody Splunk

As I meandered down the trash-laden streets, a deep voice rose from the gutter grate: "*Down here.*" I looked down there, and was startled to see a basilisk swishing its tail in the darkness. "*Before you dain to pass this gate . . .*" His voice caused tremors in the pavement. "*You must answer me this riddle.*"

"So be it," I said.

The creature spoke in a rumbling whisper. "*Large as a mountain, small as a pea, Endlessly swimming in a waterless sea.*" His eyes burned with the fire of a thousand suns. "*What am I?*"

I bit my thumb, and raised my eyes. The stars were numb smears against the engulfing void.

"You are an asteroid," I said.

The creature threw back its head and gave a roar so great it shattered the windows in a nearby warehouse. Its head spun round like a whirling dervish, and when it ceased spinning, its countenance was transformed.

"You're not a mere basilisk," I exclaimed. "You're a shape-shifting basilisk-sphinx! Never has there been a creature so rare—and so dangerous." I drew in my breath. "According to *Book IV of Engagement with Creatures of Foul Darkness*, you are honor-bound to accept my riddle. So answer me this:

Long-limbed and Learn'd,
I read, game, and snack,
Oh unquenchable longing
What is it I lack?

(See back for answer, Ms. F.)
Answer: Janice Gibbs won't go out with me.

How the Vampire Resolved the Global AIDS Crisis

by Julie Chang

I guess he turned everyone with AIDS into vampires. Then, because they were vampires, they would live forever. And not die of AIDS. But I guess then there would be the problem of all these AIDS vampires spreading disease when they sucked people's blood. So maybe it would be better if the vampire just did AIDS awareness education. He could go around to assemblies in high school cafeterias and tell people about AIDS and show them how to put a condom on a banana, like you did in homeroom after Kristi got pregnant, Ms. Freedman. Except no one would laugh, or ask *what is the difference between an erection and a boner?* or say it didn't look like you'd ever opened a condom wrapper before, because you kept fumbling, and you finally tore it open with your teeth. Everyone would just be really frightened, and use condoms, and not get AIDS.

How the Cephalopod Balanced the National Budget

by Andy Lopez

Cephalopods seem like mystical creatures to me, Ms. Freedman, because they have no vertebrae, and they can change color faster than a chameleon. Also, I was wondering: are those your real eyes, Ms. Freedman? Because there's a lot of light in them, when you stand by the window. I thought maybe you wear contact lenses, and that's where you get those little flecks of green. If the Cephalopods balanced the national budget—I am thinking here of lots of tiny slugs jumping on calculator buttons to do the equations—you wouldn't have to buy us scissors and tape. And you wouldn't be so stressed, because we would have more books than just *Reading is Fun!* from 1972, which as you pointed out, is for fourth graders. You wouldn't have had to bring in all your childhood books from your family's basement, and you wouldn't have been so upset when someone drew boobs and a penis on Black Beauty. I know you think it was me, because of those notes I wrote you, but it wasn't. I wouldn't do something like that, Ms. Freedman. I like you. I think you're the best teacher in the school.

How the Pegasus Created World Peace

by Amelia Basil

I rode the Pegasus to school on Monday morning, and we stood on Ms. Freedman's desk and testified to the rapturous power of the Lord. The Pegasus interpreted scripture and I spoke in tongues. Angelica Masterson fell to her knees and saw a vision of souls tormented in lakes of fire. She abandoned her way of darkness, and no longer made me swallow erasers in second period. Then the seventh seal was opened. The sun turned black, the moon became blood, and stars fell to earth like fruit shaken from trees. The Lamb of God appeared in all his glory, his white robes blinding our eyes. I knelt before him, and he put his hand on my head. "Well done, good and faithful servant," he said. A sword of joy pierced my heart, and I felt the violence of love.

How the Succubus Got Me Laid

by Phil Gasher

I was lying on my bed, staring at these pictures I ripped out of *Playboy* and taped to my ceiling. I wanted it bad. My little brother, who shares my room, was like, "Wanna play Legos?" And even when I looked at the Lego princess, who is tiny and square and yellow, I felt kind of turned on. Suddenly, the room began to shake, and the Lego princess grew a pair of bat wings, and then she grew bigger and bigger until she was this really hot, tall, yellow woman, only with goat hooves and a forked tongue. Due to my comic book wisdom, I recognized her as a succubus, which is a female demon who seduces men and draws away their life force. I was like, Davy, go downstairs, I need to have some personal time with Lego princess.

I lost ninety percent of my life force that afternoon, but it was totally worth it. And that is why, Ms. Freedman, I kept falling asleep in class last week.

How the Wood-Nymph Saved the Environment

by Janice Aurelia Gibbs

It would be kind of like that time that you brought in cupcakes on your birthday, Ms. Freedman, and Andrea Shylomar said they tasted like wet bananas, and you were like, "Very well then, Andrea, give me back the cupcake," and she was like, "No, miss, I was just saying stuff, I'll still eat it." Then Danny Ramirez was all, "This frosting looks like poop." And you lost it, Ms. Freedman. You took his cupcake and smashed it against the chalkboard. The cupcake stuck to the chalkboard for a few seconds, and when it fell off, it left this smear on the chalkboard. Which, Ms. Freedman, you have to admit, did look a lot like poop. Anyway, you just stood there; breathing loudly, and then you made everyone fold their arms on their desk and put their heads down. You turned off the lights, and you sat at your desk, and you ate, like, ten cupcakes. You even ate the wrappers. We were all scared, Ms. Freedman, because you had always been so nice, and you were acting *whacked.*

Anyway, it would be a lot like that with the wood nymph. At first everyone thinks, "We can do whatever to the environment, she won't even do nothing." For a thousand years, the wood nymph forgives us for destroying the world. But when someone cuts down the oldest and tallest redwood tree, her patience snaps. Big-time. She makes the plants wither and the volcanoes explode and freezes the water to ice. Which really makes people think about their behavior. Then maybe they change.

How My Dad Fixed the Lawnmower

by Adam Sandoval

I guess my Dad is kind of like a mystical creature, Ms. Freedman, because he died when I was three. I guess he would be like a ghost now or whatever. Like an angel or a spirit or something. Anyway, I was thinking, what if he came back? My mom would be so happy to see him, she would kick Trent out right away, and say *I never want to see your ugly face round here again, my husband has come back, and he's not going to give me thumbprint bruises on my arms, or lie on the couch all morning putting out cigarettes in cartons of ice cream.* My dad would be a light blue kind of color, filmy and electric. Not just him, but everyone who died and had families missing them—they would all get to come back. Everything that was broken would be fixed, Ms. Freedman, they would even find your journal, which Danny Ramirez hid under the dumpster behind the gym, but don't tell anyone I said that. Everything that was lost would be found.

How the Phoenix Got Ms. Freedman Out of Texas

by Laura Freedman

The phoenix appeared at Ms. Freedman's window.

"You're crushing the gardenias in my windowbox," she said.

The massive bird groomed its wing.

"You may as well come in." She patted her bed. "Have a seat. Can I get you a drink?"

The phoenix shook its head.

"I was planning to have Raisin Bran for dinner," she said, sipping wine from a coffee mug. "But if you're hungry, I'll thaw some chicken."

The phoenix cocked its head to the side.

"Don't look at me like that, bird. I don't need your guilt trip."

The bird widened its eyes.

"I mean, why *should* I stay?" Ms. Freedman gestured with the mug. "Are you going tell me that I'm sowing 'seeds of hope that may take years to sprout'? That I'm reaching them in a way that's 'invisible but real'? Because I've been telling myself that all year, bird. I don't need to hear it from you."

The phoenix regarded her in silence.

"I feel like an empty yogurt container with a banana peel stuffed in it. I mean—can an empty yogurt container with a banana peel stuffed in it transform a child's life? No."

The phoenix fluttered to the windowsill.

"It can't even be recycled."

The phoenix cocked its head to the side. Beckoning.

Ms. Freedman stood up and stepped to the window. She nested her fingers in the phoenix's plumage and hoisted her body onto its back. She burrowed her face in its neck. She could feel its heart reverberate against its downy skin.

The phoenix stepped into the windowbox, crushing a gardenia. Then it thrust out its wings, and flew.

BRIDGES

Psychiatric Wellness Solutions

Warm Greetings, Laura Freedman!

You are an honored guest here at Bridges: Psychiatric Wellness Solutions. We hope you find that our Wellness Points™ system offers a uniquely effective approach to emotional optimization. Our founder, Dr. Sherman Weir, developed the capitalist model of cognitive behavioral therapy when his son was diagnosed with schizophrenia. Frustrated by the limits of traditional inpatient therapy, Dr. Weir envisioned a system where enlightened self-interest drives positive behavioral change.

How Do I Earn Wellness Points™?

Guests earn Wellness Points™ by participating in activities that activate emotional optimization. Guests can use Wellness Points™ to pay off their Emotional Debt™ and rebuild their Psychiatric Credit Score™.

Mood Chart	+10 Wellness Points™
Water Aerobics	+10 Wellness Points™

Jungian Clay Modeling	+10 Wellness Points™
Journaling Therapy	+10 Wellness Points™
Sand Play	+10 Wellness Points™

What Can I Buy With My Wellness Points™ ?

Macrobiotic Cookie	10 Wellness Points™
Hot Tub Soak	20 Wellness Points™
Letter	25 Wellness Points™
Visitor	100 Wellness Points™

Are There Behaviors I Should I Avoid?

Crying jags	-25 Wellness Points™
Name Calling	-25 Wellness Points™
Passive Aggression	-25 Wellness Points™
Aggressive Aggression	-100 Wellness Points™

(List not exhaustive. Further penalties may be enforced at staff discretion.)

When Do I Get Out?

To obtain an approved release, you must rebuild your Psychiatric Credit Score™. Your recent BIPOLAR BREAK WITH CONSENSUS REALITY has lowered your Psychiatric Credit Score to 0.

Can My Wellness Points™ Accrue Interest?

After maintaining emotionally productive behavior for one week, your Wellness Points™ enter the Wellness Portfolio™, where they maintain 5% interest.

Can I Gamble With Wellness Points™?

On Casino night, with staff approval, guests may gamble with Wellness Points™.

Can I trade food for Wellness Points™?

No.

What Now?

By checking in, you've declared Emotional Bankruptcy™. Time to start rebuilding your Psychiatric Credit Score™! Consult the activity schedule in the lounge for your first Wellness Points™ activity.

Spirit Engaged,
Andrew Schaffer
Outreach Coordinator

✯ THE UN-GAME ✯

Dear Ms. Freedman,

We kept asking Ms. Campos why you abandoned us after break. She said you had "health issues." Phil Gasher says he knocked you up, but barely anyone believes him, especially the part about it being the medical miracle of Siamese twins. I kept bugging Campos until she ripped a kid's drawing off the bulletin board and scribbled your address. *Ms. Laura Freedman, Bridges, 900 Pecan Blvd, Austin, TX.* At first I was like, ah, shit, Ms. Freedman's a druggie! Because a cousin of mine went to a rehab called *Bridges*. On the home page, though, it says, "Guests unwind in the whirlpool, contemplating the exquisite beauty of arid plains." Which sounds like a super-deluxe getaway spa. Then I used my critical reading skills, like we practiced with the toothpaste ads. I realized: you are in the looney bin.

I feel bad, Ms. Freedman. Plenty of teachers have thrown a terrarium out a window and shouted, "You're driving me crazy!" But you're the first who actually followed through. You were so nice to us, too. You gave us extra credit for wearing costumes on Halloween, and you brought in all that cardboard so we could make funny hats. I don't know if you remember, but I made mine a pope's hat. I wore it after school to confirmation class, and even Sister Gloria tried it on.

The substitute we got is not so nice. The Sir. He is really into discipline. The first time Adam Sandoval sassed him, The Sir screamed, "Drop and give me fifty!" We watched while Adam tried. He barely made twenty. We felt bad for him, Ms. Freedman. We pretty much shut up and did our work after that.

While school is not so great, I got promoted at *Elysian Grove*. Kind of. I am "temporary activities coordinator," while the real activities coordinator gets a gastric bypass. Instead of wiping butts, I wheel old people into a room with moldy encyclopedias and tall windows to read "Dear Abby" and the horoscopes. Last week I taught poetry. "The Haiku is an ancient art form," I read from a printout. "It contains three lines, in a syllable pattern of 5-7-5:

Ancient silent pond
Suddenly, in jumps young frog!
Splash! Silence again."

The old people sat there. Carl started eating a crayon. Finally Jean—who is in the rest home at fifty for getting fat and depressed and not taking her meds—scrawled out some lines.

"Jean," I said. "Care to share?"

She scraped back her chair, and read:

"There once was a maiden from Norway
With ladyparts wide as a doorway.
Said her very first lover
When this was discovered,
'I guess then we'll just have a four-way.'"

I did the only thing I could do, Ms. Freedman.

I led them in a round of applause.

After ten minutes of poetry failure, the walkers up and left, and the cripples asked to be wheeled back to their rooms. I looked at the blank papers and broken crayons. So much for my plan of including old people poetry in *El Giraffe*, the Joseph P. Anderson High School Lit Mag. I thought it could add variety. Being the student advisor, Ms. Freedman, you know we get mostly suicide poems. I thought old people might write on different themes, such as tarnished lockets with pictures of dead babies, or gout. I am hoping to God that The Sir doesn't replace you as *Giraffe* advisor. I have such weak-ass arms, Ms. Freedman, and I can only do like two push-ups, so he'll probably fire me as editor and choose someone in JROTC, like Julie Chang.

Anyways, I have still been writing poetry a lot, even though you're not here. I included a poem I just finished. It is called *Eclipse*. I thought maybe if you felt like it you could read it.

Your friend,
Janice Aurelia Gibbs

Dear Janice,

Thank you for sending me your poem, *Eclipse*. I was impressed. Your journaling exercises were always strong, but this poem demonstrates a clarity and awareness that is new and exciting. I especially liked the lines, "Does the darkness hide/ the verses written in your eyes/ the spots upon your soul?" And I was impressed with the narrative turn at the end. "I walked with you for a while/ But soon I found that I / prefer to walk in the light." And nice use of enjambment! You do remember the term? Come to think of it, I'm not sure we made it to enjambment. I think our last literary term was simile. There were no similes in your poem.

You will have to forgive me, Janice. My memory is a bit shaky these days. It's not professional of me to go into this, I know, but I feel I owe you an explanation. In short: there are some pills I take to balance my brain chemistry. In November, I flushed them down the toilet. I had an initial rush of energy—I imagine you recall the lit-term *Jeopardy* board coated with industrial-grade glitter glue (I've been told The Sir burned it in the gravel pit). Soon, though, I felt a strong need to curl in the fetal position in a dark, enclosed space. Towards the end, I hallucinated that a great bird appeared at my window and wrapped me in its downy wings.

My brother tracked me down to Phoenix, Arizona, where I'd been sitting on a park bench, feeding hamburgers to birds. He brought me back to Austin and checked me into *Bridges*. The doctors have gotten my medication straightened out, but I still wake up each morning feeling exsanguinated (look it up).

I want you to know Janice, that, though I had a hard time managing the classroom as a whole, I do care deeply for each of you. It means a great deal that you've taken the time to write. Your nursing home story made me smile. To the orderlies at *Bridges*, I must seem like one of your intractable charges—I refused to attend clay modeling class three times this week. Do keep sending me poetry. I have a lot of time on my hands, here, and I'd rather spend it reading your work than filling out my mood chart.

Fondly,
Ms. F

Dear Ms. Freedman,

I'm glad they got you on the right pills. I looked up exsanguinated and it means, "drained of blood and life." I feel that way a lot of times when I get home from work. Maybe I need some mental meds and a week at *Bridges*, ha ha.

In order to waste time at the rest home on Thursday, I inventoried the supply closet. As I counted crates of tangled string and stacks of brittle magazines, I realized: the "supplies" are just things old people leave behind when they die. Gross. Then I saw the "Un-Game," battered in the corner. I thought: damn, a real supply. An activity for tomorrow!

Me and the Un-Game, we go way back. I first played it at Amelia Basil's house. Amelia's parents believed in exact fairness. They liked the Un-Game, because no one wins. You just take turns pulling question cards like *Who do you trust?* and *Which is your favorite: triangle or dodecahedron?* While I played the game on Amelia's rug, shoveling Cheez-Its in my face, I learned that Mrs. Basil's happiest moment was eating jumbo shrimp dipped in cocktail sauce a week before her wedding.

This seemed sad to me.

Today I wheeled the old people onto the sun porch to play the Un-Game. Aurora leaned down to pick up the lid of the game box. Her eyes wobbled. She put the box on top of her head.

"It's to shade myself," she said.

"Do you want me to get you a hat from your room?"

She held it there, arm shaking. "I have no hat."

"Okay," I said, feeling bad she had Parkinson's, plus also a box on her head. "You can go first." I flipped through the deck, discarding downers (*Share a big letdown in your life. What do you think it's like after you die?).*

"Okay, Aurora. I found one for you!"

It was hard to watch Aurora's emaciated body tremble. It was like watching a grandma be crucified.

"What is your most sentimental possession?"

“My Bible.”

“A classic! What’s your favorite story?”

“The cripple at the well.”

“I like it when Jesus overturns the tables in the temple and drives out money-changers with a whip of braided cords.”

Aurora nodded grimly.

I turned to Helen, whose body swelled out of her wheelchair like a rising mound of dough. “Helen. *What advice would you give a young man about to get married?*”

“Buy her . . . flowers,” Helen croaked, trying to adjust her thick, terminator-style shades.

“That’s sweet. Did your husband buy you flowers?”

“My lover . . . did.”

I imagined a lover climbing Helen’s mountain of flesh, planting a flag in her perm. “Good for you, Helen. Way to seize the day.” I turned to Nancy, a frail woman with skin like dried apples. “Nancy. *What are you most proud of?*”

Nancy brushed an imaginary crumb from her arm.

“Like, what have you done in your life that you feel good about?”

She rubbed her eyes.

“Nancy. C’mon. Participate.”

Tears ran down her face. “I’m not proud of anything,” she sobbed.

So much for the Un-Game.

Before I worked here, I thought living a long time would automatically make you kindly and wise. Not so much. The old people cheat at bingo and throw hissy fits about toast. Anyways, I’m going to see if I can steal some beer from my aunt, and get wasted, and forget about my day. Don’t tell.

Your friend,
Janice

P.S. This is a kind of weird poem I wrote on my break today. It is called, *Nicoli, Who Was Thrown To the Wolves Behind the Sleigh, 1845.*

Dear Janice,

I suppose I don’t have to tell you that your prefrontal cortex is not fully formed until the age of twenty-five. Abusing alcohol in the teen years may cause your brain to re-circuit, wiring you for dependence on alcohol or other substances.

But I understand why you'd want to drink. Sometimes the mind whirs and pinwheels, rising and contracting on roller coaster stairs, and you need a little something to blur the flashing lights to shade forests of tree green.

At least postpone your drinking until you make it to college. Please. Alcohol could be your camel's straw—the weight that tips you into the world of perpetual rest home employment. Try that for purgatory.

Sorry I'm jangly. They've augmented meds, seeking that which won't exsanguinate. This new cocktail (of drugs) makes me feel I've swallowed batteries. Energizing yet artificial. I do not recommend.

Naptime!
Ms. F

Dear Janice,

I haven't heard from you in a while, and I worry my last letter offended you. If so: apologies. It's hard for me to tell, sometimes, when I should staple back my tongue. Your choices are your own.

As for your poem. What a strange, lovely opening. "You used to pet the/ soft fur that grew on the tips/ of my ears. Pleasure in the seat of my belly/ as you held me, mother." I wonder if you might consider adding one more verse. As it is, it's a bit difficult to tell exactly what happens after the mother wanders into the snow. Overall though, fine work.

Best,
Ms. F

Dear Ms. Freedman,

Sorry I didn't write. It's just I found out the Smucker's plant is closing down. My dad is being transferred to Piggott, Kentucky, which just happens to be where his jam factory girlfriend (Glenda) was transferred six months ago. According to the brochures, Piggott is famous for hand-carved wooden canoes and Kentucky's only life-size wax museum. I HATE WAX FIGURES! I screamed, throwing a light fixture at my dad. THEY ALWAYS COME TO LIFE AND TRY TO KILL YOU! According to him, that's not the point. According to him, he can't get another job here, unless he works the fields, and his back can't take that. The worst part is, he wants me to stay here, and live with my fat aunt. He says it's because I'm already in school here, but I know it's because Glenda doesn't want me living with them. So now I get to share a room with my cousin Macy, who is always saying things like, "Planning on growing boobs this year, Janice?" Plus, she is pregnant, so I am also going to be sharing my room with a screaming baby. God. I hate my life. Maybe I could come be your roommate at *Bridges*. Ha. Ha ha ha ha. Seriously, though, I'd rather live pretty much anywhere than with my aunt.

Cross My Heart & Hope to Die,
Janice

Dear Friend of Laura Freedman,

This letter is to inform you that, due to the complexity of this therapeutic juncture, *Bridges Psychiatric Wellness Solutions* has deemed it best to isolate our client from outside stimuli. All mail for Laura Freedman will be returned to sender until further notice. Thank you for your concern.

Spirit Engaged,
Andrew Schaffer
Outreach Coordinator

FROM: janthepiratespy@hotmail.com
TO: lfreedman@anderson.edu
SUBJECT: ?!?

Dear Ms. Freedman,

I am e-mailing you because maybe you will get a chance to sneak away from a nurse and look at your e-mail. They are not giving you my letters because you are apparently on lockdown. God, what did you do, assault an orderly? Jesus. I looked at the *Bridges* website again and I have to say the place creeps me out. First of all, who signs *anything* "Spirit Engaged"? Second, the section on electroshock therapy says "To ameliorate the stress of temporary memory loss, *Bridges* staff eliminates potentially stressful stimuli." Which I am thinking means you are getting electroshock therapy. God. I didn't think they even did that anymore. Does your hair stick out crazy all over the place? I hope you're okay. I really hope you're okay.

Your Friend,
Janice

FROM: janthepiratespy@hotmail.com
TO: lfreedman@anderson.edu
SUBJECT: RE: ?!?

Dear Ms. Freedman,

I guess they are not letting you check your e-mail. Who knows, maybe they don't even have computers there. Maybe it's "excessive stimuli." Ha ha. Well guess who is teaching our English class this year? The Sir. Yes. Principal Gutierrez liked the way he licked us into shape, so she hired him full-time. We are learning lots of literature under this totalitarian regime, if learning lots of literature means filling out worksheets while The Sir paces the room, bristling. I have to admit, though, it's kind of cool to see him shut down the cocky kids. Even Danny looked nervous when The Sir made him stay during lunch hour for a "conversation." I was lounging on the grass, drawing a yeti on my jeans, when Danny stumbled out of the classroom. He looked like he'd been through a wind tunnel.

"Did he get you with the bullwhip, Danny?"

"He made me clean out the hamster cages."

"What does that have to do with you throwing a stapler at Timon?"

"He accused me of 'inciting irresponsible reproductive activity among rodents.'"

"*You* put Arnold Shwarzehamster in Tulip's cage?"

"I wouldn't have done it if I knew that bitch would eat her babies."

"Dude, you deserved what you got."

Danny looked me over. "Janice. Way to get boobs this summer."

I flipped him the bird. I was about to let that punctuate our conversation, but then I thought, hey. You know what would serve my dad right? If he heard I was hanging around with losers, such as Danny, who has been in my class since kinder. Back then he had a head like a T. rex, and he brought his toys crashing down on my head without reason. My dad hated him.

"What are you doing right now?"

"Ditching P. E. and taking you to the lake?"

"The last time I hung out with you, Danny, you cut the hair off all my troll dolls."

"Aw, Janice, come on. You're too old to play with dolls, anyway."

So I went to the lake with Danny. On the way we stopped and got Slurpees and when we got to the lake we poured rum in them and they were cold and good as we sat on the hood of his car. When you get to know Danny, it's surprising. Beneath the cocky asshole exterior, there is a sticky marshmallow interior. We reminisced about old times, like when Adam Sandoval choked on a golf ball in second grade and the janitor saved him. Danny told me that his dad always wanted him to be a doctor. He worked night shifts at the Discount Mattress Outlet to save for Danny's college, until he had a heart attack while stacking kings. They found him the next morning, hands clutching his heart. Dead.

"You should be a doctor, though, J. You were always smart and stuff. You could be one of those pretty doctors like on TV."

"Not if I keep failing."

"You do good in school."

"Um, The Sir's P. E. class?"

"Smart people suck at sports. It's like, one of those inverse scenarios."

"Wow. It's like you were almost paying attention in math."

"You probably just suck at push-ups because you have brains in your arms instead of muscles." Danny drew a diagram in the mud with a stick. "Actually, your boobs are probably all filled with brains, too." He added two wiggly lumps to his diagram.

"If I have brains in my arms, how am I about to punch in your face?"

"You're the doctor." Danny flicked the stick into the lake. "Don't ask me."

Don't worry, Ms. Freedman. I'm not stupid enough to get knocked up like Kristi Colimote. I just want to hang out with dino-head enough to freak out my dad.

Xo
Janice

BRIDGES

Psychiatric Wellness Solutions

Journaling Therapy I: *The struggle to adjust to a new or stressful environment can lead the emotionally labile to a psychiatric 'break.' Where were you before you came to Bridges? Describe that location in detail.* (10 Wellness Points™)

Name: Laura Freedman

I got used to searing heat hitting my face like bricks from a bread oven. I got used to waking up covered in sweat, nightgown sticking like moist Saran Wrap, used to treating sun-scalded arms with ice and aloe. I got used to pickers on ladders: arms dashing in and out of branches, faces shaded by hats, necks laced with kerchiefs. I got used to the scent of orange blossoms mixing with the smell of hot dirt and moist grass, to round and dripping globes seared open at every meal, to pink-flushed interiors flaunting themselves on our secondhand tabletop.

I got used to the *colonias* bordering the groves: unincorporated regions with faulty electricity, where people lived eight to a trailer or a shack. I got used to walking on the side of the road in the track of a tractor's tread, averting my eyes from dead dogs and smeared cats, watching children bouncing like beans on a trampoline, creaky church speakers splaying salvation—prayers and threats, chants and tambourine songs. I got used to God incarnated on every street corner—used to lugging soiled clothing to Waters-of-Life Laundromat, where tracts delineating the plan of salvation are taped to the top of the dryers, used to buying pink-frosted cookies at De Dios Panaderia—the Bakery of God.

I got used to students who whispered to each other in a language I caught flecks of—students who had crossed the river, or whose parents had crossed the river. I got used to students from Guatemala, El Salvador, Nicaragua, Mexico, Peru. I got used to barbequed corn spread with mayonnaise, squeezed with lime, sprinkled with chili. I got used to kids pooling quarters for cokes, pickles, and paper boats of Flaming Hot Cheetos drizzled with nacho cheese.

I got used to birds: small black birds flying up from behind a building like God had tossed up a handful of currants, birds squalling in the parking lot of the grocery store (drowning the hum of industrial refrigerators), chachalacas—brown robed nuns to the spangled disco dancer peacocks—cackling in the dust of our yard. I got used to the chatters, squeaks, squalls, peeps, calls that sounded like bitter laughter, whistles, flutes, calls that sounded like souls ascending to heaven. I got used to dust and flatness, to sunsets like pink water pouring from the sky, flooding the earth with orange soda. I got used to wind: the hot, cruel wind of afternoon, the merciful magnolia breeze of night.

I got used to it.

But then I had to go.

P.S. Dr. Bin Ladin: I know you have my letters. GIVE. THEM. TO. ME.

✯ I HAVE BORNE WITNESS ✯

Monica has long curly hair, which always looks wet, and she is wearing a shirt that says: STOP . . . *pretending you don't want me.*

She arches her thinly plucked eyebrows. "Guess who won't stop asking for her cigarette?" She takes her time card from its slot and punches it in the paint-chipped metal machine.

"I'd better go and give it to her," you say, reaching up to tighten your ponytail. But your ponytail isn't there, because you cut off your hair with a pair of baby blue safety scissors last Tuesday, when your car was parked by the creek. At first you thought: I'll stuff it all in an envelope and mail it to Dad, as a joke. But then you looked at the lilies cropping up from the thick ragged vines by the creek and you wanted to go pick them, so you thought: I'll toss it all in the creek, and the water will carry it downstream. So you got out of the car with your hair in handfuls, and it stuck to your arms because of static, and you left the car door open and you slogged through the vines to the creek bank, and then you remembered that instead of rushing brown water, there were just puddles in the creek. So you arranged all of your hair in a puddle, let it float there on the scummy water, and you thought: if some owls dive down and take my cut-up hair for a nest, I'll have done at least one useful thing in my life.

"Janice?" Monica stands in front of your face, drawing you back to the creamy yellow walls of the *Elysian Grove* staff lounge.

"Oh," you say. "Right. Shirley, cigarette." You swing the door open, and burst into the hallway.

The *viejos*, you think to yourself. They will not bring me down.

You discover Shirley sitting on the leather couch by the doorway, next to the nurse's station. "Shirley!" you cry. "My poppet! My princess!" You throw open your arms and stride towards her. Shirley's brain is fried from Alzheimer's. She pops up, propping herself with her rolling rocker.

"Do you have my cigarette?" she asks, animated in her powder-blue leisure suit.

You tear around in a drawer in the nurse's station until you find Shirley's cigarettes and a hot pink lighter. "I *do* have your cigarette," you say. "Let's go outside and *smoke* it."

Shirley wheels her walker onto the sunny, splintery, porch, and sits in a plastic deck chair. You plop down next to her and shake a cigarette out. You hold the lighter while she inhales, widening her eyes cartoonishly. "Thanks babe," she says. Then you light one for yourself.

Jean limps onto the porch in her pink nightgown, plods down into a deck chair, and stares at her feet. All the skin on her body droops and hangs, wads of fat sucked away by a staff-enforced diet. Her jowly face is gray around the corners of her lips. She looks at Shirley, frowning.

"If I ever get like that," she mutters, "Shoot me dead." You look at Shirley, who is staring out at the parking lot like a perky bird. "She doesn't even know who she is." Jean thickens her eyebrows. "It's disgusting."

You remember when the mental home across the street came over for Bingo, wearing seizure helmets, watching you with squinty gentle eyes. Jean got in a fight with one of them. A 'tard called her out on stuffing lucky bingo boards in her sweat pants, dishonorably winning rows of Sara Lee nut brownies. You didn't care, because you had the keys to the prize box. You ate all the brownies you wanted, secretly unwrapping them under the table, covering the crinkle noise by cranking the bingo wheel, sneaking bites between calling out numbers.

"The nuns at my church told us not to kill ourselves," you say, leaning back in the plastic deck chair, crossing your legs.

"Lots of people do," Jean says, widening her eyes, convicted. "When someone wants to, you can't stop them."

"You're a pretty lousy friend if you don't try." You crush your cigarette out in the cement ashtray, smearing black ash into brown sand.

"I was on the boardwalk," Jean says. "In San Diego, when I lived down there. I was walking on the beach at night, and a girl came up to me. She was crying, and she told me that her beau had made her pregnant, and wasn't going to help her out."

"I know the type."

"And she said that her parents would throw her out if she told them." Jean shakes her head. "There wasn't anything she could do. She told me she was going to drown herself."

"And you saved her, Jean. You stopped her," you say, like a calm psychologist. You know how psychologists talk. You have seen the compelling specials on *Lifetime*, television for women.

"I couldn't." Jean winces. She flicks her cigarette and stares at the shadows made by deck chairs. "She just walked into the ocean." Jean stands up. She leans heavily forward on her cane, dingy pink nightgown swinging, and plods off the deck.

Shirley sits up alertly. "Can I have my cigarette?"

"Sorry," you say. "We're out."

"Dammit!" Shirley squawks, pounding her fist on her powder-blue knee. "I want my cigarette!"

"Not now. It's dinnertime."

"Am I cooking?"

"Yes. Everyone's here." I lower my voice. "*And they're hungry*."

"Shit," Shirley mutters, lifting her walker up slightly and clanging it down on the porch. "Shit." She surveys the deck, conspiring escape.

"Let's go to the store and buy a ham hock."

She raises her head, yellow eyes brightening. "Okay!" She leans up, turning her walker towards the ramp. You jump from your chair and feel for change in the soda machine. You bound over to the doorway, and in. Monica is sitting with her feet up on the desk, phone cradled against her ear, laughing.

"I'm taking Shirley for exercise," you whisper, edging the cigarettes and lighter onto the desk. Then you chase down Shirley, who is on the edge of the nearly empty parking lot when you catch up.

"Shirley-babe. Shirley-my-man."

"Where are we?" she demands, confidentially irritated.

"We're going for a stroll." You lead Shirley out of the parking lot. You walk with her through the neighborhood with gravel streets and plastic toys on yellow grass, corn growing over fences in back yards, screaming kids on trampolines.

"Let's talk about our lives," you say to Shirley, strolling over broken glass. "What's new with you?"

"I don't know," Shirley says, frowning and dismissive, shoving her walker over a weedy sidewalk crack.

"Personally," you say, surveying telephone lines and an armless doll lying on a roof, "Personally I say we go to the park." So you walk Shirley to the park, where an *abuela* in a black and brown flowered dress is sitting on a metal bench. She has the arm-folded resignation of someone in a knitted black shawl in the sun, as she saggily watches her grandkids or her daycare run around the grass. You never met your own *abuela,* your dad's mom. But you inherited skin that browns but doesn't burn and her first name for your middle one: *Aurelia.* Janice *Aurelia* Gibbs, an ugly name-pretty name sandwich. Janice and Gibbs are choppy block sounds, no good for poetry, but *Aurelia* sounds like moving water. At coffee hour after mass, the Mexican ladies laugh that English is good for directing animals, but God prefers speaking Spanish. Ha! No wonder God doesn't answer your prayers.

You leave Shirley's walker outside the short wooden wall of the sandbox, help her step up over its dusty top, holding her thin-skinned hand. You walk across little dunes and mountains to the swing set, turn her around, and push her down in a swing.

"Okay," you say. "Let's swing." You lean back and kick your legs forward, pressing them together. "It's like we're kids again," you say to her, swinging by on a short pendulum of wind, but she is just sitting there gripping the iron links, looking at the sand, surreptitiously skeptical. You swing up, higher, swinging out of this park, out of this town. You are swinging away, swinging some place where things move fast and people talk back to you.

You dig your feet into the sand and rock forward and back, digging trenches as you slow to a stop. Shirley is still staring around the playground, not quite approving. She turns to you, agitated.

"I forgot to pick up the kids," she whispers, face cross-hatched with guilt.

"I picked them up already. I got them."

Then you look at her and think—what if she slips off the swing and breaks her face? You'd have to explain it to Chip, your manager, who has puffy red skin and brings six Dr. Peppers to work each day in an ice cooler.

"C'mon" you say to her, and stand up and pull her up off of the swing, and you walk back across the hills and gulleys of sand, over the wooden wall, across the ratty grass to a metal bench. You sit her down and lie on your back on the bench next to her, squinting your eyes in the sun.

Shirley scans the playground. "Those your kids?"

"No, thank you." You crack back your knuckles. "No kids for me." One more year of high school, then you will leave your home. Be history. Goodbye, Janice. Janice has left the country.

The *abuela* at the next table is giving out purple grapes to her kids. They are scrambling around the aluminum table like vultures or ants, crawling on top of it, then one of them shouts something and they run off for the field. They shouldn't run with grapes in their mouth, they could maybe choke. You know this, you babysat when you were thirteen and keeping it together, putting away dollar bills and dimes in a sock under your pillow.

The *abuela* looks up at you, and you nod, because you are both babysitting here, daydreaming while keeping care of others, lives on hold. She stands up, calling her kids back in, to go home and take naps, or watch TV maybe. She looks at you, and plucks up a bunch of grapes from the watery Saran Wrap.

"*Uvas*?" She dangles them questioningly.

"Sure," you say, reaching out, and she drops the cold dusty blue grapes into your palm. "Thanks."

She smiles at you, showing front teeth framed by metal dental work. Her kids swarm up to her, and they leave the field for some place cool and shady. You hold out a ripe-split grape for Shirley, and as she reaches to take it, you catch sight of a silver charm-chain on her skinny wrist. "That's a pretty bracelet," you say.

Shirley looks down at the chain, and you realize: it is a medical bracelet. Like the kind that warns if someone is allergic to penicillin.

"Oh, this?" she says, dismissive. "I don't know where this came from." Frustrated, she fumbles at it with her thumb and forefinger.

"What does it say?" you ask. You squint down at the line of script carved into the metal.

Engraved are the words, "*Do not resuscitate.*"

Shirley squints. "I can't read it," she mutters.

You pluck a grape, and place it in her palm.

"It just says your name," you say. "It just says, 'Shirley.'"

✯ THE TURNIP ✯

BRIDGES

Psychiatric Wellness Solutions

Journaling Therapy II: *Tell us about your father.* (10 Wellness Points™)

Name: Laura Freedman

FUCK YOU, Dr. Bin Ladin.

Stocks

After Vietnam, my father opened an auto body shop, and entertained his ample intelligence playing with stocks. He slipped the family savings into unstable markets, agitating our mother, who wanted the money for curtains, for furniture, for life. Looming destitution unmoored and enraged her. When her emotions riled, he clasped her arms, and shouted, "Pull yourself together, woman!"

A few years after he lost everything in the stock market, she hung herself in the garage.

My brother Steven was eight. I was four.

My father started over, and his portfolio grew. He papered the wall of his office with stock charts, tracking markets with colored tacks and string. He invested in Walmart and Halliburton, and tended his garden of money until it bloomed. Still, he stole toilet paper from the library and ate from dented cans.

Oatmeal

Wearing his navy sweat suit, he stirred gummy oatmeal, fried expired sausage on the stove. In the oatmeal pot went diced apples, raisins, milk, butter, brown sugar. He scraped a spoonful of peanut butter into each of our scratched white plastic bowls, handed us mugs of hot chocolate floating with marshmallows. We stirred as they melted, fizzing, dismembering into froth.

The Poor

At nine, I asked my father if he believed in God. He told me priests in Mexico frighten the poor from using birth control, thus they multiply. He had seen the garbage pickers when he traveled down the coast to walk the beaches and collect seashells. Starving. Half-naked. Living on trash heaps. Better off dead. All the poor should be sterilized, he said.

"And who would get to decide who would be sterilized?"

My father laughed, somewhat stumped. "I would."

"Hitler had the same idea."

"Maybe Hitler was onto something."

Rocks

On trips down the coast, my father gathered rocks. He ran them through his tumbler, subduing their edges, coating them with gloss. He glued a pock-marked, honey colored stone to a copper clasp, threaded it through with a chain, and gave it to me for my eleventh birthday. It was pretty to look at, large and clunky to wear. I nestled it in my jewelry box until the chain grew tangled, the stone unglued.

Pomegranates

My father had a suburban square of flat backyard, crabby with grass, crowded with trees. Plano's heat made branches heavy. The pomegranates were so ripe they split open, revealing red, finger-staining seeds. In college, a burgeoning paper sack of the fruit inhabited a corner of my dorm room, staining the carpet, perpetually threatening mold. Straining for connection, I wrote my father postcards singing its praises as a midnight study snack.

Conversion

Calling from my dorm room, I told my father I was tutoring prison inmates.

"They'll con you," he said.

"A lot of them have really turned their lives around. They've had transformative experiences. Conversions."

"Do you get paid for this?"

"This is the best thing in my life right now."

"People don't change, Laura."

"Not with that attitude," I said, and hung up.

Losing It

"I'm feeling mentally low," my father said, and burst into tears. So Steven drove the five hours to Plano, where he found our sixty-four-year-old father pacing and crying in the driveway. A series of mini-strokes had shorted out his brain, unmoored him in an agitated cavern of dark. My brother took him home, where he buffed his heels with an exfoliating stick until he drew blood.

Walmart

At the hospital, we take turns sitting with him. I am twenty-two. A volunteer program is about to shunt me off to teach school in a dusty border town. I am ready to obliterate the achievement gap, to dismantle the systems of structural oppression and racism that plague our society, to equip leaders of the future with the academic tools to live out their full personhood.

I am liberally brainwashed, according to my father.

Desperately, I try to think of something about my future that will please him.

"Daddy," I say. "I talked to the principal at that school I'm going to work for. And she said the town has the highest-grossing Walmart in the United States."

"I'd like to see that Walmart," he says. A tear runs down his face.

What Is the Lesson Here?

If your main hobby is accumulating money, and your religion is capitalism, the end of your life will be hard. No. The end of life is hard for everyone. Maybe I should say: if your patron saint is Ronald Regan and you reject the weak and the poor, the end of your life will be steeped in sorrow. The end of your life will be unbearable.

Please Note

I'm not trying to get my father to choke down a communion wafer before he dies. That's not important. What I want for him is to experience some kind of opening outward. A healing. A sense of peace. To experience the humming lake of love beneath our feet.

Dostoevsky, Give us Some Hope

In *The Brothers Karamazov*, Dostoevsky tells this story:

A stingy old woman served only herself, save this—she once gave a turnip to a beggar. When she dies, the devils whisk her to the lake of fire, where she cries for mercy to her guardian angel. The intercessory spirit petitions God, who says: take that turnip, see if it will drag her out of hell.

The angel extends the turnip, the old woman grasps hold, and—in a twist of grace—it yanks her from the flames. The old woman cries out in relief. A smoldering soul grabs hold of her ankle, is fished from the lake. Another soul grabs that ankle, and so on, ad infinitum, until a whole chain of souls is flying up to heaven.

"My turnip!" the old woman shouts, when she sees linked souls looping behind her. She kicks. She thrashes.

The turnip breaks. They all fall back to hell.

Mercy Has Crept In

Would a necklace of pockmarked, honey-colored rock pull my father out of hell? A pomegranate? An expired sausage?

I think: yes. All these things would work. I believe that every good thing counts.

The more difficult question: Would my father kick at the wretched souls clasping his ankles?

Probably.

✯ NICOLI, WHO WAS THROWN ✯ TO THE WOLVES, 1874

FROM: janthepiratespy@hotmail.com
TO: vivaloslonghorns956@aol.com
DATE: Thursday, Sept 1, at 3:02PM
SUBJECT: what's up?

Hey Dad,

Just thought I'd send you an e-mail update. I hope things are good at the jam factory. I hear you're working on the low-sugar line. I guess that will let Smucker's tap into the diabetic/overweight market. Maybe you should send Aunt Deb some samples. Ha.

School is going great, except that I have a D in Chemistry. Also, I keep forgetting my uniform and my English/PE teacher The Sir knows not mercy. The good news is I can now do five push-ups in a row. Whoopeee.

Do you remember Danny Ramirez? The kid with the dino head? I've been tutoring him after school. I go over to his house and we shut the door to his room and just study for *hours*. I tried to invite him to dinner. Aunt Deb said, "If he wants to eat with us in front of the TV I don't give a shit." Sometimes (and by sometimes I mean all the time) Deb is in a bad mood. I think she's upset because Macy keeps sneaking out at night to blow truckers behind the overpass. She keeps inviting me to go with, but I'm just like: Excuse me, Danny and I are sitting here on my bed and doing complex math equations, so could you please not open the door at this juncture?

Well, that's all my news! Hope things are great in Kentucky! Give Glenda my love!

XOXO
Janice

FROM: vivaloslonghorns956@aol.com
TO: janthepiratespy@hotmail.com
DATE: Friday, Sept 2, at 8:07PM
SUBJECT: RE: what's up?

J
glenda says kentucky state = good nursing program. think about yr future.
will send jam.
lv dad

FROM: janthepiratespy@hotmail.com
TO: vivaloslonghorns956@aol.com
DATE: Saturday, Sept 3, at 11:09AM
SUBJECT: life/love/oppression

Hey Dad,

I want to be a nurse about as much as I want to be a brontosaurus, and given my grade in chemistry, these are equally realistic career options. I am thinking of going into something more practical instead, like long haul trucking, or poetry.

I am Editor of *El Giraffe* (our lit mag) and this year there's an office space we get to use, with a box where students leave submissions. Unfortunately, the *Giraffe* staff are pretty much the only people in the school interested in poetics, and it's tacky to pick your own verse, and we used to just give them to the *Giraffe* advisor, which was fine when it was Ms. Freedman, but now it is The Sir, who consistently fails to understand my genius. He rejected the following on the basis of "it does not rhyme."

Nicoli, Who Was Thrown to the Wolves Behind the Sleigh, 1845
You used to pet the soft fur
that grew on the tips of my ears.
Pleasure in the seat of my belly
as you held me, mother.

This rock will drink no milk,
you cradle that which crushed his head.
Father, he who drove on, silent.
At dusk you came through the snow,
waving a branch—your eyes were wild.
At moonrise you trace them,
fingerprints I made on plaster.
Mother, you did not see—The sky crackled,
I was swallowed up in light.

I am trying to get The Sir fired. Plan B to get into my own freaking magazine is to sarcastically write dramatic rhyming poems with titles like, "Tears of Blood."

Oh, and dad, Danny and I are going out! Isn't that great! I think it's so sweet. The other night we stayed up till midnight studying. He brought me flowers the next day. The great thing about staying here in Texas and living with Aunt Deb for another year is that I can see Danny all the time!

Besos!
Janice

FROM: vivaloslonghorns956@aol.com
TO: janthepiratespy@hotmail.com
DATE: Sunday, Sept 4, at 7:05PM
SUBJECT: RE: life/love/oppression

J
you want to come out at xms? see how you like it maybe stay for the rest of the yr. will send jam.
Lv dad

FROM: glendagayle@aol.com
TO: janthepiratespy@hotmail.com
DATE: Sunday, Sept 4, at 11:02PM
SUBJECT: !!!!!!!!!

Listen up you manipulative little shit. Do you think it's good for your father to work a FOURTEEN HOUR SHIFT and then, instead of going to bed with his fiancé (that's right, fiancé, eat it, J) sit awake on the sofa IN THE DARK worrying about his daughter? I happen to love this man. You, on the other hand, are raising his blood pressure with your LIES. I spoke to your aunt Deb and she has seen no sign of any "Danny." She says this "boyfriend" is imaginary. Also: I tried to go out with your dad to O'Shanigan's last night, have some fun, eat some fish sticks, maybe try a $3 margarita, and he spent the whole time worrying about how you USED to be a straight A student and NOW you're doing bad and maybe he made a MISTAKE to have you live with your aunt. Well, little miss, I checked with your school and you are passing all but PE. So. I know what you're up to. You want your dad to send for you. Well. Why don't you just try. You can see if you LIKE living here with me. I have some VERY STERN ideas about disciplining children.

LOVE, GLENDA

FROM: janthepiratespy@hotmail.com
TO: glendagayle@aol.com
DATE: Monday, Sept 5, at 4:02PM
SUBJECT: good one

Dear Glenda,

I can't remember the last time someone called me a hilarious nickname like, "manipulative little shit." You know, if I forwarded your e-mail to my dad, I bet he would find it just as funny as I did. We have very similar senses of humor. Thoughts?

Xo
Janice

TO: janthepiratespy@hotmail.com
FROM: glendagayle@aol.com
DATE: Tuesday, Sept 6, at 11:31PM
SUBJECT: RE: good one

Dear Janice,

Okay. So I went a little overboard. It's just: I love your dad so much. I don't want anything to come between us. I know you're his daughter, but you've always hated me, even though I was better to you than your good-for-nothing mother ever was.

Also: I check his e-mail account for him. He does not even remember his own password half the time. Delete! Delete! Delete!

Speaking of your good-for-nothing mother, she e-mailed him the other day. Found him on the Smuckers website. First contact in nine years. Delete! Delete!

FROM: janthepiratespy@hotmail.com
TO: glendagayle@aol.com
DATE: Wednesday, Sept 7, at 3:58PM
SUBJECT: RE:RE: good one

Glenda,

I am willing to make a deal with the devil, which is you, because it is straight up evil to delete someone's e-mail at will. But if you give me my mom's e-mail address, I promise not to come live in Kentucky. I will stay here in TX with my aunt.

Honest Injun,
Janice

FROM: glendagayle@aol.com
TO: janthepiratespy@hotmail.com
DATE: Wednesday, September 7 at 10:00PM
SUBJECT: RE:RE:RE: good one

Done.

marcia@glitterbobs.com

FROM: janthepiratespy@hotmail.com
TO: marcia@glitterbobs.com
DATE: Thursday, September 8 at 2:03PM
SUBJECT: Hi from Janice Aurelia Gibbs

Dear Mom,

Hi. This is Janice. Your daughter. I am sixteen. I still live in TX, but dad moved to Kentucky as I guess you deducted. I'm staying with Aunt Deb, or as I have dubbed her, "Vortex of Hormonal Rage McGee." I work at a care home to earn money so I can one day go away and be around some people who (unlike Deb) are excited to be alive.

How about you? Dad would get all lockjaw when I asked. I do know from neighbors etc. that you left with Glenda's husband Ray, who left behind a vast collection of commemorative plates. Glenda kept smashing them in our driveway until Dad went outside and told her *stop it already*. Fast forward ten years: they're engaged.

When I was nine, Grandpa wrote and said you'd visited him with a half-sister. A baby girl. Then we didn't really hear from you, which kind of sucked, especially when Grandpa died. He was so nice. I remember when he came to visit after you left. He took us out to lunch at Happy Garden and let me have his fortune cookie. When I knocked my drink on Glenda's lap, he told me I had the spirit of the Comanche warrior.

Anyways, now you know what I know about you, and you can fill in the rest. Also: what is a glitterbob? Is it like some kind of hair product? Do you work in a salon? I'd love to hear back from you as soon as you can write. Deb's place isn't so great. Dad's fiancé has kind of taken him away from me, so it's nice to get you back right now. :)   Okay, well, write me soon!

Xo
Janice

FROM: marcia@glitterbobs.com
TO: janthepiratespy@hotmail.com
DATE: Monday, September 12, at 2:19AM
SUBJECT: Re: Hi from Janice Aurelia Gibbs

Janice Baby,

I can't believe I'm hearing from you after all this time!!!!!!! It lifts me up, honey, like a weight gone from my back. I apologize for not being the best with correspondence. Some of this has to do with your dad telling me he'd break my face with an iron skillet if he ever saw it again. I felt bad, so I tried to step back from his life, Give him space for healing.

I want you to know that I really do love you. Fate just took me on a different path. I could stay in Texas and can jam for all eternity, as your father was content. Or I could be with the man I loved, explore the country and, you know, really *live*. This was the dream. Unfortunately, in Reno, Ray developed a certain relation with cocaine. I was pregnant with your half-sister Casey when he got sent to jail. While incarcerated, he cut out some guy's eye with a chicken bone. I thought it best to sever ties.

After Casey I knew I could never return to Texas. If your dad met Ray's baby he might smother her, like how lions kill each other's babies on the Discovery channel.

Casey is now in sixth grade. She makes good grades. When I look at her I have a pain in my chest because I am seeing her grow up and I did not get to see this with you.

Darling, I am using the computer in the break room, and my shift started twenty minutes ago, so I got to go.

All my Love,
Mom

P.S. Glitterbob's is where I work! (casino)

FROM: glendagayle@aol.com
TO: janthepiratespy@hotmail.com
DATE: Wednesday, September 12, at 9:28PM
SUBJECT: RE:RE:RE: good one

Dear Janice,

I wanted to write you again because I realized I went a little too far. It wasn't right of me to blackmail you into not coming out. It's not that I would mind seeing you. It's just you acted ugly to me. You scratched my eyes out in photographs and poured dish soap on my lemon cake. Once you threw a cat at me! Can you blame me for fearing that if you came out, you'd stop us getting married? But if you promise this is not your intent, I welcome you. (I have talked over this with my prayer group, and they think it fair.)

I also repent I gave you Marcia's e-mail. What you need to comprehend is that your mother is not a person upon whom to rely. Example: She got bored with your dad's quiet way. She got bored with being a mother. She started making eyes at my Ray, and made up some kind of big crazy love story in her head. While I knew by then that my husband was no good, I watched your mother take him away before my eyes. When she left with Ray on his motorcycle, she was laughing and throwing back her hair. I was shoving his things out the window, slamming my head against the wall.

Ray, in case you did not know, was your dad's best friend.

Your father is a good man and I pray that you model your life on him.

Love in Christian Friendship,
Glenda

FROM: janthepiratespy@hotmail.com
TO: marcia@glitterbobs.com
DATE: Thursday, September 13 at 2:05PM
SUBJECT: RE:RE:RE: Hi from Janice Aurelia Gibbs

Dear Mom,

I wonder how well you remember Glenda Gayle. Ray's ex-wife? She apparently is not your biggest fan. But she has always been pretty uptight, so I'm not surprised.

It's really interesting for me to hear the story of your life. It's way more exciting than my life so far.

In youth group this year, Sister Gloria Castillo is doing a cooking and confirmation class. Yesterday we made mini Southwest cornbreads with veggies from the community garden. Mine would have been pretty good, only I forgot the baking soda (sin of omission) and just for the hell of it shook in lots of cloves (sin of commission). Sister Gloria broke a filling biting into a clove. We stood there, watching her root around in her purse for a pain pill. "What should we do?" we asked.

"Discuss suffering," she said. She swallowed the pill dry, coughed, and sat down by the window.

The official story, suffering-wise, is that this lady eats some fruit she's not supposed to. Then God's like: good job ruining the world, you're voted out the garden, oh, and have fun giving birth. Most of us don't think the real God would be like that. Some of the kids think suffering teaches us to be grateful, which I said was bullshit, referring to Exhibit A: nursing home. At the end of the meeting, holding her jaw, Sister Gloria said suffering is a mystery.

It's weird that, after five thousand years of working on this, the official answer is: We don't know. Really. We have no fucking clue.

Anyways, I was thinking I might come out and see you, maybe during Christmas break. I looked up the price of a bus ticket to Reno, and it's not that bad. What do you think?

Love,
Janice

The boy wanted a do-over, so he got a job as the night janitor at NASA. He studied the stars, mapping the sky, searching for black holes and neutron stars. After years of calculation, he re-programmed NASA's most promising spaceship, and shot himself towards the black hole at the center of our galaxy. A wormhole spat him out, and his spaceship splashed into the ocean. After floating in an escape pod for several days, he was hauled aboard a freighter ship. "What year is it?" he demanded. "2072," a tattooed sailor said.

It was the same year he'd left. *I may as well jump back into the ocean*, he thought. What the old man didn't realize was that his calculations were mistaken. Instead of sending him back in time, the wormhole sent him to a parallel universe. As fate would have it, this was the universe in which the girl loved him back.

When the ship got to shore, the old man realized he was not, in fact, in his own world. So he tracked down his parallel universe self. His doppelganger was sitting on a porch swing in Montana, holding hands with the girl, who had been his wife for fifty years. They were drinking lemonade and watching their grandchildren play in the yard. The old man stood in the cornfields, absorbing the family happiness of his twin.

He considered murdering his doppelganger and slipping into his place. He could play tiddlywinks with his grandchildren; sleep each night next to the woman he loved. It would be easy. He'd dig a deep hole. Bonk his second self on the head with a shovel. Steal his clothes. Push the body into the pit, shovel dirt on his face.

No, the old man thought. He turned, and wandered out toward the open road. *It is enough to know that among the infinity of universes, one contained for me a chance at love.*

✯ THE HOLY INNOCENT ✯

There is something silent and filled with sunlight about this bathroom, maybe because you are alone in it, and you can breathe. Creamy white paint has been smeared along the sides of the window and over the metal crank that opens it. You twirl the crank open and look out at the decaying stucco houses and the empty fields beyond.

There are bits of glue stuck to your fingers, from making construction paper bookmarks with spaz-brains from H wing. You look down at the glue on your skin and remember youth group, when you used to smear glue on your hands and let it dry, then peel it off in flakes.

In the church basement, you used to make these tattoos on yourself. You tipped backwards in your chair on the thick pea-green carpet, writing on your wrist while Sister Gloria sketched non-violent communication spheres on the chalkboard. The first time you smoked with Danny, he licked his thumb, and rubbed it on your wrist.

"You don't have paper, there, or what?"

You shook your head, watching mallards stick their beaks down in the muck for weeds and worms.

Stupid Danny. He worked at the discount mattress factory. His boss wouldn't let him rip off mattress-tags in the warehouse, so he cut the tags off of everything else: your sweater, your book bag, your underwear.

You unbutton your jeans and sit down on the cool porcelain, looking at your tattered, scribbled-on high tops. They are the shoes you were wearing when you found out about the baby, from a test kit you bought on the way home from school. A baby in your belly, you'd thought, looking at the tab coming up blue for positive. An uninvited guest, unfurling in your stomach like a weed, a vine, a tree.

"I did not invite you to grow here," you'd said to it, tracing your finger across your belly. "I did not invite you in."

You took the baby to see all of the things in your life you wanted to show it: through the lining of your belly. You walked with the baby through the rutted, unplanted fields, you showed the baby: these are clods of dirt that grow in the sun, these are the white worms that squeeze their way up from the earth. These are the grasses by the creek. You showed your baby the secret places that only you know.

Your baby. You showed it your world and then you said: Out with you. Enough. You are out of here, you nosy little thing, I did not invite you here, get out—you fungus, you infection. I am giving you nothing, you said—touching your belly—you little mist of yeast, you rabbit, you grub, curled up with a big head like a walnut. And the baby went. You starved the little fucker out.

When you stopped eating, things slowed down. You slowed down too. You sat at your desk and you sat up as straight as you could. You sat up as tall as you could. You were waving back and forth. You drifted away on a plank and nobody knew this, which was fine, because it was your secret. It was for you to know and for no other person to know. You had a pain in your gut when it started, the baby coming out. Sharp pain like the first time you got your period, and you tried not to crumple over. You raised your hand to get out of the classroom, to go and sit in the cool bathroom stall and let it out. But when you stood up, you fainted. Then they gathered around you, and you peered up at them, like trees in the sun.

You pull up your pants and button them and bust open the bathroom door. Gazing down the empty blue-carpeted hallways, you decide to go and check on Helen, in the B wing. You need to kill an hour before you go home to your aunt's house, where you've lived since your Dad got transferred to Kentucky. Your dad worked as a mechanic on the line at the Smucker's plant, and he used to bring home little packets of grape and strawberry jam, the kind you get with your breakfast at Denny's when you order toast. Now your dad mails you shoebox packages with actual jars of jam wrapped in Styrofoam peanuts, on Christmas and your birthday. When you were twelve, you used to eat jam with spoons for breakfast and tuck lumps of it in your sandwiches at lunch. Now you hate jam. You hate its slimy sweetness; you hate how it has no flavor or bite. You'd rather have dry naked bread, hard-crusted, chalky-making to your mouth. The sweetness of your own spit is better than your father's stupid jam. You don't tell your Dad this, of course, you don't tell Dad anything. Really, you never did. He was always preoccupied, silent, nothing you said ever seemed to really go into his head.

Helen's room is at the end of the "B" wing. Her nephew pays extra for her to have a single, plus pockets of special attention time from the aides. Helen weighs three hundred and seventy-two pounds, and she cannot move by herself, except for her left arm.

You knock before entering her room. It is dark and silent. A breeze flaps at the curtains, and they rustle against the sill.

"Helen?" you whisper. She is sitting in her Lay-Z-Boy with eyes half-closed, throat gurgling, and you can't tell if she's sleeping or awake.

Her eyes flap open. "Janice," she croaks hoarsely. "I need . . . to pee."

Your timing, as always, is dead-center wrong. You wheel over the automatic lift machine and hook her hulking body into it, press the button to lift her up and set her on her plastic wheelchair toilet.

Man, you think to yourself, as you step outside her room, giving her a sliver of privacy. You lean against the wall with your arms folded, already hearing the tinkling and plopping. You look down at your shoes.

Really—it was better for your baby not to be born, then, with the kind of life it would have had. You could not hide a baby where you hid the other things, in the toe of your sneaker, in a box on the top shelf of your closet. No.

Your baby can come back to your womb another time, its soul can come back later, when you are older. When you have left this town, when you have left this state, when you have a shady tomato garden and chimes on your porch. You will be one of those older pregnant women with fine muscles and sun-browned skin. Your baby will grow inside you again, bright and strong, and it will come out kicking, so glad you made it wait.

But maybe it doesn't work like that, with souls and all. Maybe your baby just went to limbo, and is stuck there forever.

"Janice," Helen croaks from inside her room. You hoist her back up from the toilet with the machine. It's strange to lift a person up like that, to lift a dead weight of a person with a machine. You wipe her soft hanging ass and replace her diaper with a new one, sticking on the plastic tabs. Then you pull her black stretch sweat pants up and set her back down in her chair. You rinse out the removable bucket from her wheelchair toilet, running water over it in her tiny bathroom, looking at the glass bottle of sand from Florida perched on the windowsill.

You think of when Sister Gloria brought your youth group to the beach. It was the day after you took the pregnancy test, and you hadn't eaten anything for dinner the night before, or lunch that day. The sky was shining pink against the water, eddies of foam were rushing and crashing beneath the wind. There had been a storm, and the dunes were peeled bare by sweeping storm waves.

The other kids were running around in the uprushing froth of waves, rolling up the legs of their pants, throwing sandballs. Sister Gloria stood next to you on the sand, taking off her high-waisted jeans. Underneath, she wore a pilly black bathing suit. In that bathing suit, she seemed more naked than anyone you had ever seen. She walked into the water, straight on, up to her waist. Then she just stood there, letting the waves hit her, staring at the trail of light on the water leading out to the sky.

You sat on the sand, tracing a circle around yourself with a piece of driftwood. You were still deciding what to do. When Sister Gloria turned and came back in from the water, she wrapped herself in a brown towel and sat next to you. The other kids in the youth group were whipping each other with strips of seaweed. There was a dead seal on the beach next to where they were playing, and when they got too close to it, sand flies jumped from its decaying skin.

"Sister Gloria," you said, the wind paring your voice down to softness, "Where does a baby go? When it doesn't get born, I mean."

"Where do you think it might go?"

"Heaven. Right? Like God's sending a baby to hell."

"We can never overestimate God's mercy."

"But the real rules? Like, with the Pope and stuff?"

"Some theologians say that the unborn dead become companion martyrs to the Holy Innocent."

"The Holy Innocent?"

She popped a seaweed pod with her thumb and forefinger. "Are you pregnant, Janice?"

"Sister Gloria! You know I'm not stupid like that."

"Just meditating upon mortality?"

"Yeah. That seal over there is my inspiration."

Companion Martyrs to the Holy Innocent—not such an awful job. And it seemed like with being a nun and all, Sister Gloria would be right.

But Sister Gloria was wrong about a lot of things. You, for instance. She thought that she'd get you out of your mess of a family with beatitudes and liturgical dance, but instead you brought the mess with you. You pierced your belly button with a safety pin in the girl's bathroom, rolled a joint with a page from Deuteronomy, and drank sacramental wine until you threw up in the community garden. You dumped dish soap in the courtyard fountain of the Virgin Mary, and on Halloween you put fake blood running down in tears from her cheeks, so that for two days everyone thought there was a miracle.

"Janice," Helen croaks to you from your chair. You've been spacing out again.

You finish rinsing out the removable toilet-wheelchair bucket, then sit back down on her bed, hands wet.

"So," you say to Helen. "What's up with you?"

Helen sits up slightly in her recliner, her sleep-crusted eyes half-drooping, her mouth open, her wrinkled forearms spotted like toads. Hoarsely, she confides that she finds the weather humid, the Mexican cook erratic with spices, her children neglectful, the staff abusive.

"Hmmm," you say. "That sucks."

While Helen speaks to you about her actress-niece's wedding (held in a theater), you flap through her photo book from her years in a retirement community in Florida. Pretty tame, all of it. Lots of pictures of social hours—tables of brownies, old ladies in dresses, poorly composed shots of condominiums and misty pink sunsets.

You snap the photo book closed and look at the pictures hanging on Helen's wall. One of them is a black-and-white photograph of her youngest daughter. Helen's told you before—she died in a car accident.

"Helen," you say. "What do you think happens to us when we die?"

"The bugs eat us," she croaks.

"You don't believe in heaven and hell?"

"The bugs . . . have to eat something . . . so they . . . eat us." She gestures slightly with the arm she can move, straining.

"Even kids? The bugs get them, too?"

"Everyone," Helen says, her eyes running with intensity.

"But you believe in *souls*. We all have souls."

"No," says Helen, her voice ragged. "When you die . . . you die."

You watch Helen's fish eyes, opened wide, watering in nests of wrinkled skin. "Are you *afraid* of death?" you finally ask.

"No," says Helen. "I wish for it . . . every night." Rivulets of water well from her eyes, and her mouth is gaping open. You don't know what to do.

"Tell me about your daughter," you finally say. You nod at the wall. "The one in that picture on the beach. What was she like?"

"Like you," Helen says.

You look at the picture of the girl. She is standing in a swimsuit at the beach, arms folded, hair wisping out of a bathing cap.

"She had dimples," Helen croaks. "Like you."

You make a corner of your mouth smile, press your hand into your cheek, feel the indentation.

"She was a pistol," Helen says.

"A pistol?"

"You're too good for this place," Helen croaks. "You belong in school."

After clocking out, you walk home—past the bakery that sells *quinceañera* cakes, the discount video palace, the wedding supply store displaying grey-skinned mannequins swathed in gauze. You pass the elementary school where your aunt works. She is home making dinner right now, you know, boiling a pot of chicken. You know that soon you will be sitting on the couch with her, chewing on chicken bones, watching television. You pass the gas station where you stopped this morning and drank three cups of coffee from a paper cup, drank until you could not keep your hand from shaking, until coffee sloshed over the top of your cup onto your fingers.

You cut through the Portuguese cemetery, dragging your feet through gravel, reading names carved in cement. Some barred, raised tombs with diamond-shaped stained glass windows line the part of the cemetery closest to the road. At the far end is a new cement mausoleum. You walk over to inspect it. It is like the cubbies you had in grade school, six coffin-spaces high and wide, waiting for the new dead.

You touch the bottom coffin-slot with your scribbled-on toe. You squat down and lean in. There's a couple of dried oak leaves that have blown inside, and it's kind of damp in the back.

You stick your head further in, stretch your arms out, and wiggle yourself inside. You roll over on your back. You can hardly hear the cars as they rush down the road. The ceiling is a chalky white. It's not so terrible in the tomb, kind of calm and quiet.

The cement is making your shoulder blades cold. It could make all of you cold. If you lay here long enough, you would be paralyzed, nothing in you would move. Then, the worms would come. They would say: we've already met your baby, Janice. And now we are meeting you.

God you say. God. I have something to say to you. Can I have this baby back? Can I have its little soul? God. Please.

You listen.

Nada.

You close your eyes. You set your cold hands under your shirt, shocking the warm skin of your stomach. Through your palms, you can feel your blood moving, your heart beating. Your body: alive.

Your baby will find you. Your baby will find its way back home. You will say: I have made a place for you here. Climb in, my love. Now you will be safe. All is well here, my love, my darling. My darling, my own.

✯ FIRST THE SEA ✯ GAVE UP HER DEAD

BRIDGES

Psychiatric Wellness Solutions

Journaling Therapy V: *While Bridges subscribes to a post-Freudian therapy model, we believe that dream analysis may enable repressed emotions to emerge. Please describe the last dream you can remember.* (10 Wellness Points™)

Name: Laura Freedman

First the sea gave up her dead. They floated upwards in their olden clothes, clammy, the color of clay. We hauled them upwards with nets and laid them on the coral shore. We waited for them to wake up. Rumors of war came from the East. A terrible thing in the water. Nobody wanted to watch as the skin of the earth swelled up like a blister and let what was in there out.

Bones it was. Mostly. We couldn't see them moving, but each day they drew themselves closer to whole creatures, joints meeting and knowing one another as kin. The priest said the earth was tired of people. It was spitting them out like bad fish. Expelling the poison of men.

When our hair grew faster, we knew time was speeding up. The film reel cranked faster to end this ugly picture. A woman gave birth in a cave in the mountains. She was out hunting truffles. She had been only three weeks with child.

I grew breasts and began to bleed. They dressed me in white and tied a list of their sins to my back. They sent me to speak to God. God, who is invisible, prefers no place to another, but is equally distributed within each grain and drop. I sat on the beach and picked a green leaf from a green plant. I spoke to God in the leaf. "You who can do all things," I said. "We would like more time." The leaf said nothing. Or maybe it said everything, which, as all colors make white, sounds like nothing. On the beach, the dead were moaning. I watched them rise. The trees pulled themselves from the ground and walked hand in hand with the dead. There was nothing to do but follow.

I held the leaf in my pocket. When we reached the center of everything, the dead called out to God. I raised up my hand. The leaf was dry and gray. "Sheep and Goats," I said. "Separate." The trees knew they were good. The people were more shy. "How do we know?" they asked.

"Everyone is welcome," I said. "And there will be no more time."

✯ MEXICO FOXTROT RIDES AGAIN ✯

FROM: splunkmiester@yahoo.com
TO: janthepiratespy@hotmail.com
SUBJECT: EMERGENCY!!! ALERT!!!!

Dear Janice,

Terrible news: Ms. Freedman is being held against her will in an INSANE ASYLUM! We must rescue her before she is lobotomized! I have the keys to Greebo's car, a map of Austin, and a crowbar. I need an accomplice on this journey, and as Andy Lopez is at tuba camp, YOU ARE MY ONLY HOPE.

Urgently,
Cody

P.S. How are you doing? What is new with you? I am starting at Texas Tech in the fall! I am super excited!

FROM: janthepiratespy@hotmail.com
TO: splunkmiester@yahoo.com
SUBJECT: RE: EMERGENCY!!! ALERT!!!

Hey Cody,

Just so you know, your e-mail made you sound a little crazy. Life tip: avoid writing in all caps. It puts people off.

While I'm aware that Ms. Freedman is in a nut ward, I'm skeptical about the lobotomy. And what makes you think she's being held against her will? I admit that from the website, the place seems new age and creepy. I do kind of wonder why she hasn't written back to my emails for like a year. I'm pretty sure they're giving her electro-shocks . . .

God, maybe you're right. Not about the lobotomy, but about her being kind of trapped there. Maybe we do need to go rescue her. I mean, not really rescue her. But just check in?

~Janice

Jailbreak!

A True History by Cody Splunk

The day dawned coarse and muggy, red sun on the rise. Red sun means bloodshed, my father always said. I took a final drag on my fizzy caffeine pick-me-up. Swearing an oath that the blood would be that of our enemies, I crumpled the can in my fist.

With a sudden, jarring, door slam, my partner in crime emerged from her abode, almond eyes flashing, black hair twisting in the breeze. Janice was a full plate of spaghetti—personality for five packed into one supple frame. And yet: her Yeti jeans had loosened since I'd seen her last. She was all angles. I added a secondary mission to the quest-o-meter: fatten Janice up. Fifteen minutes into our drive, I swerved into a Dr. Butterbeans.

"Just coffee," Janice said, lighting a cigarette.

I ordered two extra-large breakfast specials.

"Sure that's healthy, Splunk?"

Driving with one hand, I tossed breakfast in her lap. "Something to soak up the coffee."

Janice stared at the bacon cool ranch burrito, then flung it out the window. "I have a problem," she said, as it splattered against a fire hydrant.

"Apparently."

She took a yellow notebook from her bag. *Laura's Journal of Mystery and Wonder*, the cover read.

"*You* stole it?"

An open case, closed—with my partner in crime the culprit.

"It was Danny."

"Of course." Danny, the perpetual villain, always managed to slip through the fingers of the law. "When?"

"That day Gasher got his hand stuck in the computer screen."

Chaos—a perfect cover for crime.

"How'd you get it from Danny?"

"It was under his mattress."

"You're still seeing him?"

"What's it to you?"

"He treated you like shit, madam."

"I treated you like shit, sir."

"You were going through a hard time."

"That's no excuse." Janice extinguished her cigarette on her shoe. We passed a billboard that read: HELL IS REAL.

"So how's the rest home?"

"I wouldn't put my hamster there."

"You have a hamster?"

"They fired me. For smoking patients' cigarettes."

"Harsh."

"Well, I also ate one lady's diazepam."

"That's like a German sweetbread?"

"It's more like valium."

"So does Freedman know you have her journal?"

"Dude, I got it yesterday."

I swerved, almost veering into a ditch. "You were with Danny *last night*?"

"Cody! You are not my boyfriend!"

"Is Danny?"

"None of your business.

"You're throwing your life away like a rancid pot of stew!"

"And you, my friend, are a terrible driver."

I steadied the vehicle. We passed a porno store. Lurid posters obscured the windows. 24-Hour DVD! TRUCKERS WELCOME!!!

"Anyway," Janice said. "Fill me in on the genius rescue plan."

"Behind you."

Janice turned around in her seat, inspecting my array of supplies. "You recently join the circus?"

"Those are our disguises. You're going to wear the wig, sunglasses, and raincoat."

"Is the plan that I expose myself on a playground?"

"When they bring Ms. Freedman out to see us, we communicate our plan through morse code blinking."

"Ms. Freedman knows morse code?"

"She's been to college."

"Where she studied *literature*."

"You and Ms. Freedman trade outfits in the bathroom. You remain hidden in the stall. Wearing your clothes, Ms. Freedman accompanies me from the building."

"How long do I have to stay in the insane asylum toilet stall?"

"That's where the rope ladder comes in. Once we clear the premises, the security system should be disabled by the super-virus I loaded onto the mainframe."

"This is crazy."

"Yes," I said. "Crazy enough to work."

A wooden sign shaped like the golden gate bridge announced our destination. "*Bridges*," it read. "*Psychiatric Wellness Solutions*." The blacktop road ended in a baking-hot parking lot. Janice jumped out of the car and stretched, riding-up tee shirt revealing starving-horse ribs. I donned a fedora, and tossed her the raincoat. "Showtime, sister."

We followed a red brick walk past low-slung stucco buildings and a tennis court with faded lines. In a fenced-in swim area, a maintenance man fished a dead mouse from the hot tub.

"Remind me to skip the jacuzzi," Janice muttered.

Inside, the air conditioning made a white-noise roar. At the nurse's station, a man typed intently. We studied the glossy printout tacked to the bulletin board above his head.

WEEKLY WELLNESS POINTS™ MEMO

Due to recent events, WELLNESS POINTS™ penalties have been expanded. Time to TAKE RESPONSIBLILTY™, folks. You have no one to blame but yourselves.

Poking an orderly in the belly and shouting, "You are plump and good for Eating!"	-10 Wellness Points™

Pretending to be deaf, and, when docked Wellness Points™, filing a complaint under the "Americans with Disabilities Act."	-25 Wellness Points™
Attempting to wager Sexual Favors On Casino Night	-35 Wellness Points™
Starting "cells" of a "Communist Party" to overthrow the capitalist system of cognitive-behavioral therapy.	-50 Wellness Points™
Nailing Dr. Sherman Weir in the eye with a paper airplane, that, when unfolded, says "FUCK YOU, Dr. Bin Ladin."	-75 Wellness Points™

"Villagers are restless." Janice pushed her sunglasses up on her nose and tapped the bell.

The bearded orderly stood, frizzy hair on end. "How may I help you?"

We're here to visit Laura Freedman," Janice said.

"I guess you should sign in the 'ol binder. Would you like a complimentary *Bridges: Psychiatric Wellness Solutions* golf pencil?"

"Absolutely," Janice said.

We signed in.

The orderly glanced at the binder and raised his eyebrows. "I'll let Laura know that Kristi Colimote and *Mexico Foxtrot* are here to see her," he said, disappearing into the back room.

Janice kicked me. "Nice code name. Subtle."

"Okay." Beardo called back to us. "Visitor's area down the hall and to the right."

The visiting room smelled like antiseptic solution. Ms. Freedman was escorted in by an orderly in a fauxhawk. Her hair was in a weird wadded up bun on her head, and her tee shirt was emblazoned with paw prints and red letters that read: MY CAT WALKS ALL OVER ME. "Janice? Cody?" She sank into a folding chair and pinched my arm. "Is this really happening?"

"We thought you were lobotomized," Janice said.

"Not yet." She gave a brittle laugh. "Ever since the Fudgesicle incident, though, they stopped giving me your letters."

"I'm starting at Texas Tech in the fall," I said.

"Congratulations."

"I can make four types of breakfast burritos," Janice said.

"Oh?"

"I work at Circle K." Janice said. "I didn't really graduate. I never got my PE credits."

Ms. Freedman suddenly looked like herself again: sober. Exhausted. "Janice." She put her head in her hands. "I blame myself."

"That's funny," Janice said, "Because I blame Cody."

"I blame Society," I said.

"I blame God," Janice said. "Who made the world, anyway?"

"The big bang," I said.

"Yet you believe in dragons," Janice said.

We sat there for a moment.

"Where are my manners!" Ms. Freedman suddenly exclaimed. "May I offer you a snack?" She removed a napkin wrapped packet from her pocket, peeled back a rubber band, and proffered a smashed cookie.

"Thanks," Janice said, taking a piece. She chewed. "Oh my God." She spat into her hand. "That's so incredibly stale."

Ms. Freedman's pale fingers tightened around the napkin.

"Ms. Freedman," Janice said. "We're here to spring you."

"I don't know about that, Wellness Points™ wise," Ms. Freedman said. "Bad debt, you know. Credit score."

"Ms. Freedman, use your critical thinking skills." Janice said.

"Like we practiced with the toothpaste ads," I said.

Ms. Freedman's eyes welled with tears.

I glanced at the fauxhawked orderly, who was dozing in his chair. "Smoke bombs at the ready," I said.

Janice took Ms. Freedman's hand, yanked slightly. Ms. Freedman stood. Haltingly, she followed Janice into the bathroom. I scouted the premises, fingering my nunchucks. Then I pressed my ear to the bathroom door. Ms. Freedman and Janice were speaking earnestly.

"I starved it out," Janice was saying. "I killed it."

"Janice. It is not medically possible to starve a baby out."

"It worked, though."

"Spontaneous miscarriage is extremely common in the first trimester. Especially with a first pregnancy."

"It would be one month old."

There was a pause.

"I'm so sorry, Janice."

"Hey. Don't start crying on me, Miss."

"Emotional lability. Minus 10 Wellness Points™."

"Anyway, your make-up's done. You look kind of good with that wig on."

"This is crazy."

"Yes." Janice swung the bathroom door open. "Crazy enough to work."

In the raincoat, sunglasses and wig, Ms. Freedman looked like a sad clown. She rubbed her eyes, smudging eyeliner. "How's Janice escaping?" she whispered.

"I've got pepper spray and a rope ladder."

"Janice." Ms. Freedman set her hands on Janice's shoulders. "I need you to promise you won't assault anyone. Aggressive Aggression is minus 100 Wellness Points™."

"Scout's honor."

"Janice will run down the highway to the gas station," I said. "Once she's there, she'll radio in. We'll swing back and pick her up."

"And get Slurpees," Janice added.

"I haven't had a Slurpee in *years*," Ms. Freedman said.

"Alright, Ms. Freedman." I took her hand. "Here goes nothing."

Schizophrenics shuffled past, minds wrapped in terrible cocoons. Ms. Freedman didn't seem to know what to do with her hands. "Do you have a cell phone?" she whispered.

I handed her my phone. Ms. Freedman held it to hear ear. "No, Gretchen," she said, animated. "I can't give you a better offer on the house." Walking aggressively, she made a beeline for the door.

I moseyed up to Beardo at the front desk. "Can I sign us both out?" I asked. I nodded to Ms. Freedman, who had her back to us. "My girlfriend's on an important phone call."

Beardo gazed out the window at Ms. Freedman's back. "You know," he said. "Your girlfriend's ankles remind me of Laura's ankles. Such slender, delicate, ankles."

"Your commentary seems inappropriate."

"Is it alright if I step outside and say goodbye to—what was her name—

Kristi Colimote? Beardo tucked the binder under his arm. "She really should sign the binder."

"Sir," I said, blocking his way. "It's a very important phone call."

Beardo stared me down. "Is it, *Mexico Foxtrot*?"

I blinked.

"Emilia," Beardo called into the back room. "Situation 2."

A rotund woman in pink scrubs emerged from the back room. "Situation 2," she barked into the intercom. Classical music started up on the PA system.

I glanced behind me. Ms. Freedman was nowhere to be seen. I made a break for the front door. As I pushed it open, I shouted, "Run for it, Ms. F!"

"I'm going after him," Beardo screamed, flinging himself at the door.

I sprinted down the red brick path, then veered left, into a courtyard filled with tiny fountains. I tore around a shed, Beardo's footsteps pounding gravel behind me. I faked a right, then sprinted across a sand garden to the parking lot, jabbing my hand into my pocket for the keys. Beardo made a dive for my feet, pulled my ankles out from under me. "Where is she, you bastard?" he shouted, sitting on my back, wrenching my arm. "Where is she?" I raised my bleeding face and scanned the parking lot. Greebo's car was gone.

Janice and I sat in dark leather chairs of Dr. Sherman Weir's office, hands tied behind our backs.

Dr. Weir wore a red bow tie and sported a luxuriant mustache. He paced the room, piercing us with a steely gaze.

"Let me guess," Janice said. "You have ways of making us talk."

Dr. Weir opened a desk drawer, removed an inkblot flash card. "Tell me," he said. "What do you see?"

"Your mom's honeypot," Janice said.

Dr. Weir flicked the flashcard like a throwing star. It stuck up out of the carpet. "Where's Laura?" he demanded. "Where is she?"

"I have literally no clue, sir. She actually stole my car."

"We were just visiting, sir. You have no right to detain us."

Dr. Weir sat on the edge of his desk, arms crossed. "According to one Max Gusterson, Laura Freedman was wearing the clothing you came in with." He poked Janice lightly on the forehead.

"Get your hands off her!" I cried.

"Listen," Janice said. "We want lawyers."

Dr. Weir laughed maniacally. "This isn't a police station. You have no rights. I've checked you in as patients."

"Patients have rights," Janice said. "In the nursing home, there was an eldercare ombudsman."

"We demand to speak to your ombudsman," I roared.

"There is no ombudsman." Dr. Weir laughed. "The complaint line goes directly to me. And complaints have a way of . . . disappearing."

Janice raised her eyebrows. "Minus a million Wellness Points for being batshit crazy."

Dr. Weir looked stricken.

"You have so many bats in your belfry they violated the building code!" I said, snapping my neck aggressively.

Janice glanced at me, confused.

"From overcrowding. Because there were so many bats!"

Dr. Weir cleared his throat. "You should know, munchkins, that you have deprived us of a very lucrative patient. Ms. Freedman was participating in an important medical trial. The pharmaceutical company will be quite disappointed." He shook his head. "If only we had a replacement." He set his hands on Janice's shoulders. "You wanted to be Laura Freedman? Congratulations. You *are* Laura Freedman."

"Oh yeah?" Janice said. "I don't even have insurance."

I struggled to free my wrists. "Our parents will come looking for us! We'll expose your conspiracy!"

Dr. Weir flipped through papers on a clipboard. "Let's see." He nodded at Janice. "Oppositional-defiant disorder, *anorexia nervosa*." He pointed at me. "Mania. Delusions of grandeur." He set the clipboard on the table. "Oh, nurse," he called musically. "Will you ready the Thorazine?"

Beardo stepped in with a tray full of needles, grinning.

"Now are you sure you don't want to tell me where our patient is?" Dr. Weir demanded.

Beardo readied the needle at my shoulder.

"Never," I spat.

The door flew open, kicked in by a canvas high top. Ms. Freedman stood in the doorway, wielding an X-ACTO knife.

Dr. Weir's mouth fell open.

Moving like lightning, Ms. Freedman jabbed the Thorazine into Beardo's thigh. He crumpled to the ground. She wrestled Dr. Weir into a headlock and held the needle to his throat. "Time for a taste of your own medicine," she whispered, and drove the needle home. He sank to the plush red carpet. "Sleeping on the job," she muttered. "Minus 50 Wellness Points™."

She slashed the X-ACTO knife across our bonds, then looped the rope ladder around a desk leg. "What do you think, kids?" Her eyes were wild; her makeup smeared like war paint. "Time to check out?"

We scrambled down a brambly hillside, where Greebo's car sat waiting in the Circle K parking lot. We bought three extra-large Slurpees, filled the tank with gas, and floored it into Austin.

Ms. Freedman's brother lived in a high-rise apartment. We paused before it, engine running.

"Well," she said, looking small and tired in the back seat. "I'm going to have a lot of questions to answer. I think I'd better go in alone."

We nodded.

"Thanks for rescuing me," she said. "I don't know how I can thank you." Tears ran down her cheeks. "I wasn't even a very good teacher."

"Yes you were," Janice said.

"You were just different," I said.

Ms. Freedman smiled sadly.

"Good luck, Ms. Freedman," Janice said.

Ms. Freedman turned, walked up the path, and pressed the buzzer. As the front door opened, it bathed her in a frame of light.

Back on the highway, it was a long time before we talked. "You didn't give the journal back," I finally said.

"No shit."

"You chicken out?"

Janice unrolled the window, letting cool air rush in. She pulled the journal out of her bag, pressed on the overhead light.

"Janice Gibbs: a feral child with excessive eye shadow and stringy black hair that obscures her face. I feel a daily urge to take scissors to it. She has an anti-authoritarian complex that would be interesting were it not so ill informed."

"Ouch."

"Yeah. But, obviously that's not how she always felt. Otherwise she wouldn't have even kept in touch, you know?"

"I guess."

"I think it's better if she doesn't know that I know she thought I was a little shit. I mean, before she knew me."

"Good call."

Janice switched on the radio, and we sang along really loud with the windows open.

It was pretty much the best night of my life.

THE END

FROM: janthepiratespy@hotmail.com
TO: splunkmeister@yahoo.com
SUBJECT: collective memory

Hey there Cody,

I read your account of our adventure with much interest. However, I remember a few things a bit differently. For instance, if memory serves me correctly, after we went up to Ms. Freedman's room, she shared that she was going to be released in two weeks. She checked out on a day pass, and we ate lunch at Burger King. Then we dropped her off at her brother's house.

I'm doing night shifts at the Circle K on North 23rd street. Stop by sometime for Funyuns. We'll catch up.

Your pal,
Janice

✶ THEIR TRUNKS ✶ WERE THEIR HANDLES

Sitting on the cold cement, Janice felt foreign to herself. A thousand years away from any city she had known. Maybe by city she meant her childhood. She could say, "We had these plastic elephant cups, one blue, one pink, their trunks were their handles." She could say that to Juan, and he would look at her, waiting for the rest of the story. Juan didn't understand. The elephant cups were a story in themselves.

Juan had the shift before her, and she would burble up with stories to make him stay longer, grabbing at thoughts like fish in a stream, blurting them out in fluorescent light. She didn't like to be in there alone in her green vest, passing cigarettes over the ad-emblazoned counter to skinny users who radiated sharp sparks of need.

She had not been a user herself, not really, not until a junkie threw a cup of boiling coffee at her face just as she was ringing up his purchase. Reeling from forming blisters, she had tripped on a box of pineapple rings, jerked something in her back. The junkie peeled all the green from the register, was out before she called 911. When the doctor stopped refilling her Percoset, she got it from a neighbor with a plastic hip. Her aunt thought she slept with the dude to get the pills, but Jesus. She had standards. Leaning on a metal bat, her aunt rang the dude's doorbell and said: keep it up and you'll have plastic elbows. In the doorway, Janice sank to the tile in laughter. *Plastic elbows.*

Her aunt stood over her, bat raised.

Go ahead, Janice said. I dare you.

Her aunt dropped the bat, sat on the couch, turned on the television. Janice got up and made instant mashed potatoes. In the glare of the flashing screen, they spooned hot, milky, ketchup-slathered bites to their mouths.

At work that night, she slipped a fifty up her sleeve.

Stupid.

Stupid.

Stupid.

The holding pen was the size of a cramped kitchenette. There was a drinking fountain with a clogged drain spilling water on cement, a metal toilet bolted to a back wall. Janice shifted her weight from foot to foot.

"Knew I'd end up here," muttered a heavy woman with a straw-colored braid. She wore a shirt that read: EVIL KEEPS ME YOUNG.

"I have that shirt," Janice said.

"I didn't realize it came in 'Elvin.'"

"I didn't realize it came in 'Elephant.'"

"You're sweating. You should take off your jacket."

"You should take off your face." A sharp pain tore through Janice's lower intestine. She bit her lip until it bled.

The large woman lowered her voice. "Are you a vampire?"

"What gave me away?"

"Bloody teeth. I'm Gwen, by the way."

"Zelda of the Night."

"Want to know what I'm in for?"

"Desperately."

"I took my daughter to McDonalds."

"Didn't realize that was illegal in Texas."

"Apparently it's kidnapping."

"Yikes."

"Yeah, well, when your baby gets ripped out of your arms and adopted by a rich bitch who sends you pictures every year, then calls and says your nine-year-old daughter wants to meet you, and you drive three hours every month to eat a Happy Meal with her, that does NOT give you the right to pick her up from school and take her to McDonalds yourself. Apparently that's kidnapping." She slammed her head against the wall. Hard.

"Jesus."

Gwen leveled her face at Janice. "I have multiple chemical imbalances."

"Go figure."

"All my hair fell out when I was four. From stress. My mom's boyfriend would chase me around the house pretending to be a gremlin."

"Sounds stressful."

"The doctors were really surprised when it grew back."

"Move it, *Mija*." An emaciated woman in heavy makeup slapped Gwen's shoulder. "I have bad knees," she explained, sinking down and sighing.

"What are you in for?" Gwen asked.

"I ran over my husband."

In the corner, a toothless woman gave a sharp staccato laugh.

"He deserved it."

"Obviously," Gwen said.

"After twenty years of marriage. I should have known from the start. I hated my wedding."

"How come?" Gwen asked.

"It was a terrible day. Before, I didn't get my period for three months."

"You were pregnant?" Janice asked.

"I was a virgin."

"Hey, I know all about pregnant virgins," Gwen said.

"I was an Ivory girl. Twenty-two years old. 98% pure."

"Keep your feet in a bucket and a penny between your knees!" the toothless woman screamed.

"And then, I got it the day of the wedding. And it was heavy. I used two, three Kotex every hour. My mom wouldn't let me wear tampons. Mexican mothers are like that. And the *crinolina* that I had underneath my wedding dress, it was all stained. Between my legs, it was messy. All streaked. And then after the wedding, we had to do that *Pinche Dinero*.

"*Pinche Dinero*?" Gwen asked.

"It's a dance, where everyone dances with the bride and pins a dollar on her dress. Mine was a five-dollar *Pinche Dinero*. When I went to change, I just left the dress there with all the money on it. It was all dirty. All brown. And then when we went for the honeymoon, I had changed into pants. And when we got out of the car, my husband said to me, 'You're stained.' I yelled at him. 'Who are you to tell me that?' And when we got inside the hotel, I locked myself in the bathroom and cried and cried. And in the morning, the bed was stained again. I came back from my honeymoon *intacto*. The same way I left."

Intacto, Janice thought. *The same way I left.*

Assigned to a cell, Janice crouched over the toilet and retched. Someone (her sleeping cellmate, it had to be) had taped a Bible bookmark over the toilet:

> *Behold the birds of the heaven, that they sow not, neither do they reap, nor gather into barns; and your heavenly Father feedeth them. Are not ye of much more value then they?*

Yes, God, Janice said, curling on cement. I am worth more than a bird, and I wish that you would sometime *act like it*. God, who so loved the world, where dreams shriveled at an astounding rate, flash stop photography fast-forwarding a flower's death. God, who promises not to keep you safe, Sr. Gloria said, but to never leave you. *My God, my God, why have you forsaken me?*

Even Jesus said it.

God is the god of the present, Sr. Gloria said. *If you stay in the present, God is with you.*

Fuck that also, Janice thought. When had the present moment ever been good? Okay, maybe here and there. Squatting on a curb sharing a cigarette, arms wrapping her after sex, the warm buzzing alcohol plateau before sobs wracked her body. Fleeting, all. The goddamn morning always came. The sun returned, blasphemous in its consistency, making her look really shitty in five-dollar makeup.

Janice curled her body around the stabbing ache in her side.

For I have been in the belly of the whale.

Her cellmate sat up in bed, looking dazed. She was a stop sign-shaped blonde in her mid-fifties with a drug-ravaged face.

"Who are you?"

"Zelda of the Night."

"Well." The woman ruffled the back of her hair. "Glad to have the company. Most of these bitches don't talk. The dying art of conversation!"

"SHUT UP!" A voice across the cellblock shouted.

"You want to sit on the bed?" She patted the scratchy gray military blanket. "We'll chat?"

"I'm cool here," Janice said, pressing her face against the metal toilet seat.

"You're probably wondering what I'm in for." The woman regarded her coyly. "I did something artistic. Something *bad*."

Janice vomited violently.

"Oh, Sweetie."

Janice wiped strings of mucus and bile from her face.

"You know that skinny bitch won't let you in the sick bay. You got to ask the night guard. The one with the prosthetic foot."

Janice wiped her face on her shirt.

"Right, my story. Like I was saying, this *yoga* studio moved into my neighborhood. And my boyfriend, he was ogling the girls when they came out. He would talk about their 'yoga bodies.' But I was like, yoga? No, I'm on a fixed income. So I went to the studio and said, "I'll take the ten classes for ten dollars." And the owner said, "Lady, I can smell alcohol on your breath." And I was like, "That is not possible, as I am wearing cologne." And he was like, "Ma'am, please leave the premises." And the next week, he installed this dark glass in the windows, so I couldn't even peek in."

"SHUT UP!" the voice down the cell block yelled.

"So I was like: okay, very rude and hurtful. And, being an artist—I was a middle school art teacher—that night I took a can of spray paint and made that glass my canvas. Modern art!"

"What did you paint?" Janice asked.

"Yoga boners, mostly. Plus some choice words for that—

"SHUT UP OR I WILL STICK A BROOM HANDLE SO FAR UP YOUR CUNT IT'LL COME OUT YOUR EYE!" the voice down the cellblock shouted.

"Guess those are the rapists," Janice said.

"Oh, no," the cellmate said. "That's just Tabitha."

For I have been in the belly of the whale.
And I came out of there intacto. The same way I left.

Except you don't come out intact, Janice thought, curled on cold cement. You come out stinking like fish. You get vomited onto the sand. Rot in the sun. Gulls tear at your flesh. Sand flies jump from your decaying skin.

Nausea rising.

There is nothing left, Janice pleaded. There is nothing left.

Janice shielded her eyes.

"So this is me hitting rock bottom?"

"More or less," the angel said.

"It feels like shit."

"Yes," the angel said.

"Please intervene."

"Yes."

"Now would be a good time."

The angel put its hand on Janice's head.

"Thank you," Janice said.

The angel heaved Janice over its shoulder, and limped down the hallway.

✯ VIRTUE OF THE MONTH ✯

I know she drank her coffee black. I know she had high cheekbones and copper hair. I know she suffered from migraine headaches, that she was diagnosed as manic-depressive, that she received electro-shock therapy.

This is my mother, Olivia Freedman. She hung herself from a rafter when I was four years old.

"I'm getting a headache," I tell Ben. I am curled against the warm window of the passenger side of his truck, knees drawn to chest.

Ben turns the radio down. We are on the fourth hour of this five-hour drive to my father's house. Ben has been singing along with the rock station, church choir tenor mingling with crackling static.

I look past his profile, at the small town traffic, the spindly palm trees whipping in the wind. Hot car exhaust mingles with the smell of gasoline and the fried, oily odor of Luby's Cafeteria-Restaurant. The sign on the buffet place has removable black letters, like a movie theater marquee. *Luby's for lent!* The sign declares. *Tilapia! Catfish! Salmon Filet!*

We roll past peeling storefronts, black iron benches, a small church. On its well-kept lawn, a sign: *Virtud de Mes: Honestidad.* "The virtue of the month is honesty," I inform Ben.

"Then tell me," he says. "What's the craziest thing you've ever done?"

A thread of images blurs my mind. Bleak and terrifying, all.

"When I was in college, I would go swimming in the fountains. By myself. In the middle of the night."

"Maybe you were a dolphin in a past life."

"I see myself as more of a hermit crab."

"Maybe we were hermit crabs together."

"In a past life? No way. You would have been a dolphin."

My mother wore dresses sewn from floursack, dresses worn until they were worn out, worn-out dresses cut to aprons, quilt squares, rags. She was sixteen in the humid Texarkana summer, canning tomatoes while her parents were in town. Water boiled on all the burners, jars sucked in their seals, water steamed up, boiled down. Olivia tried not to drop hot jars, tried not to burn her fingers, tried not to spoil the fruit. She sent her youngest brother—an epileptic—to fetch water from the open well.

He was eight years old.

He had a seizure, fell in.

Drowned.

Day two in Plano. My father's sunken living room is carpeted with ochre shag, yarn I yanked at as a child. I sit down at the piano, plunk some stale notes.

"I didn't know you played." Ben peels off his paint-flecked work shirt, flops on the couch.

"Sweetheart." I spin around on the piano bench. "Chopsticks doesn't count." Ben pulls a *National Geographic* from the coffee table, flips it open. His face is eager, searching, bright.

I don't know where he came from. Darkness rolls off him like water, the weight of the world does not grate him down. His face lights up at my voice, the mention of dinner, the prospect of sex.

"I'd kill for your endorphins," I say.

"If you want endorphins, go on a run."

"Ben. What's the worst thing that's ever happened to you?"

"In high school, I had tonsillitis so bad my throat closed up." His dimples fade. "I could only eat yogurt for a month."

My laughter comes out hard and brittle. Frightening.

"Jesus, Laura. I lost, like, thirty pounds."

"Oh my God." I rub my face with my hands. "Want to know the worst thing that ever happened to me?"

He braces himself.

I flop on top of him, burrow my face in his neck. "My boyfriend tried to make me go running."

He swats me with the magazine. "It would actually be good for you."

Thanks for doing this," I say, trying my teeth on his collarbone. "Thanks for coming with me."

"Baby." Ben stretches and yawns. "I'm getting paid."

It's true—my lawyer brother is paying us to spend a weekend preparing the house for sale. It's sat empty, gathering dust, since our father died six months back. I'm sorting photos and letters, folding clothes into boxes. Ben is painting over the peeling yellow with a tasteful tan. He is eager to supplement his income with odd jobs, subsisting, as he currently is, on parental largesse and student loans. When he finishes his MBA in June, however, he will plunge with alacrity into the world of energy consulting and economics.

"You're my favorite sellout," I whisper, and kiss him on the temple.

Olivia's mother was a grim-lipped woman, hair tightly wound. She blamed Olivia for her brother's death, radiating silent coldness, accusation wearing wrinkles in her face. Olivia left home at eighteen, lived in a boarding house, worked as a secretary. She met my father while waiting in line for peanuts at the movies.

Ten years later, Olivia was in a tract home in Plano, with two kids and her auto mechanic husband. She got word that her mother was on her deathbed, waiting to see her daughter, wanting to make peace.

Olivia got a migraine. She stayed in her room for three days, until word came: her mother had died.

I stand in the garden, watering grapefruit. Ben walks along the roof, agile and balanced, lengthening shadow echoing steps.

Standing in this garden, my mother felt a fog steam and darken her brain. Dingy loudness. Rustling like wings of sparrows.

I look at Ben, with the sunset boiling through his leather tool belt and wavy hair. I shift the stream of water towards the pomegranate tree, where unripe fruit hang stunted by frost, tiny and green.

Standing in this garden, my mother felt a fog steam and darken her brain. Agitation rose in her flesh—a feeling of fish biting her skin, water receding beneath her, a vacuum opening outward into time.

Some mornings, riled with anger, Olivia would unmake beds, stuff sheets in the washer, vacuum violently, scream at those who crossed her path. Some mornings, she gardened, whistled, let me crack eggs in a bowl and roll round mounds of snicker doodle dough. She drank, and hid beer cans behind the sewing machine. She made a scene in church. Slit her wrists in the bathtub. Inhaled chemicals in a toilet bowl. She came back from the hospital, passive and dazed. She played Euchre. She dieted. In photographs, she was pleasant, loving, laughing. Beautiful.

Ben stands behind me, drinking lemonade. Examining photographs I've laid out like solitaire cards on the table.

He taps the edge of a picture. "You look like her." In the snapshot, Olivia holds a hard-shelled suitcase in a shipyard, her floral shirt tucked into a woolen skirt. Behind her, a car hangs suspended by a crane. She is laughing, wearing lipstick.

"She doesn't look crazy." Ben frowns.

"Sometimes she was normal. Sometimes she was fine."

After six months of dating, Ben still believes that my Seroquel tablets are for epilepsy; that my shrink visits are weekly massages. I guess I seemed stable when I met him. At twenty-six, I have suede suit jackets, potted cacti on my porch, and a job teaching English to migrant farmworkers. I read more books in a month than Ben does in a year.

And this is my longest-running relationship. Other boyfriends left when I emphasized a point by throwing a bowl of salad out the window, or slapped them in the face for crunching too loudly on saltines. But my meds are better adjusted now. And Ben is more accepting, or less observant, than any other man I've loved.

In my father's closet, I find a ledger book. In the front is a record of my father's stocks. In the back, terse notations regarding my mother's episodes:

April 3rd: *3 bottles behind the radiator.*

April 7th: *O. dropped kids at Sunday school, stopped at the liquor store, bought wine. Confrontation in the parking lot.*

April 10th: *Came home from work, found her in bed, cuddling with the baby. Drunk. Liquor on her breath.*

We sleep in my father's bed. A red and brown quilt, pillows that smell like dust. I lie unsleeping in the house where migraines came to my mother, pressed in on her, crushed her until she could not breathe. The air is close and tight. The force of gravity growing. I unfold myself from Ben's arms; get up to open a window. But there are no windows in this bedroom. I stand by the bed. I stare at the wall. It is puckered with textured stucco, prickly beneath paint.

"What are you doing?" Ben asks, eyes half open. He lifts the covers with one arm.

I climb back in bed, rest my head on his chest. Spooned against the warm curl of his body, fumigation takes place. Damp toads sleeping in the cave of my chest awaken. One by one, they hop away.

Dream: The Bureaucracy of Heaven

File Clerk: No suicides.

Olivia: *(Crazed silence.)*

Me: You've got to consider her circumstances.

File Clerk: (*Lifting a stack of papers.*) Despair is the greatest sin. (*Raises eyebrows.*) The sin of Judas.

Me: Judas betrayed *Jesus.* (*Taking Olivia by the arm.*) Surely one suicide does not compare.

File Clerk: (*Glances at records.*) Peter betrayed Jesus when the cock crowed three times. Yet he stands at the gate of heaven. Judas went to hell for hanging himself in the potter's field.

Me: (*Incredulity.*)

File Clerk: Despair is the greatest sin. (*Thumbs through regulations.*) The failure to believe God's redemptive power. Suicide is a sin of despair.

Me: Then I feel sorry for Judas.

File clerk: (*Raises eyebrows, lowers glasses on nose.*) Dante made suicides into bleeding trees.

Me: (*To Olivia*) Let's go.

The next morning, I sit on the garage steps. A pink and hoary scrub brush rests beside me, a disheveled but obedient pet. My father used it to scrape duck shit from my shoes, after they'd yanked stale bread from our hands. I'd stood on the cement picnic table, surrounded by toothless beaks. Afraid.

I open my notebook. Write her a note.

Olivia:

This is the logic of suicide:
(£) Suffering > (Ω) Coping Mechanisms = (∞) Unbearable Suffering
Given: Death (Θ) = cessation of suffering
Answer: Death (Θ)

See, but what if you reduced (£) or increased (Ω)? Then:
(£)Suffering < (Ω) Coping Mechanisms = (Ψ) Bearable Suffering

Dust motes swim below the rafters. The window gleams, piercing and bright. My eyes unfocus, and Olivia appears—filmy, electric blue, muttering to herself.

I put the rope around my neck, thin and scratchy. Then I saw it, flashing, how it would happen, white clatter of light going out in my brain.

"Mom," I say, cheeks wet.

The walls assault me with their whiteness, these curtains hang at my neck like vines, I clutch at the drapes and pull them, get me out of this house.

"It's me."

Olivia looks into my eyes. She is suddenly chewing on a cigarette. Sitting next to me on the step. Calm. Exhausted.

This happens to you too, you know. She touches my cheek. *Don't worry, babe.* Her hand is soft, and strangely warm. *You've got a good year left.* She flickers, then shorts out.

Ben finds me sitting on the garage steps. He eases down beside me, bad knee cracking.

I poke at a fissure in the cement. "This house creeps me out."

Ben surveys a wastebasket of hoary tennis balls, orderly rows of tinned meat, mop heads fraying with grime. He tucks his hair behind his ears. "I found something in the crawlspace."

Ben has found a bamboo picnic basket filled with my mother's papers, wedged between fragile oriental plates and ancient barbell hand weights. We repair to the living room, and finger through a sheaf of onionskin documents. At the top: "*English 103. Olivia Freedman.*" Twelve essays from a community college English course.

"*A Memorable Day*" details a visit to the circus with my brother and me. *"Never having seen an elephant in the flesh, I wondered if the great gray creature would inspire the sense of wonder I have read of in books. I was not disappointed. The clown's antics delighted Stephen, and I could not help but join in his laughter. Laura, however, was frightened by the shouting and clanging, so I fed her with peppermints . . ."*

"*The Most Interesting Person I Know*" offers a description of me at three years old. "*While Stephen was at his first day of school this fall, I had busied myself in the kitchen, cutting the crusts from Laura's sandwiches. When I called Laura to the table, she was nowhere to be found. Fearing she had wandered away, I searched up and down the street. I finally found her a block from the school, cuddling her kitten. She said that Mischief wanted to learn the alphabet, too.*"

"This isn't right." I hand Ben "*My Favorite Object*," "*An Oriental Wedding*," and "*My Recipe for Cheese Biscuits*." "She sounds like June Cleaver."

"What did you expect? *I Hurt Myself Today to See If I Still Feel*?"

"It's phony. It's not *her*."

"You were four when she died." He sets his hand on my knee. "How would you possibly know?"

"Trust me, I know."

"She's not *you*, Laura."

Hairs prickle on my neck. "What's that supposed to mean?"

"You're mad her essays aren't like pages from your diary."

"My *diary*?"

"You left it open on the dresser, Laura. It was an invitation."

"I trusted you!"

"Not enough to tell me you take anti-psychotic medication."

"They're mood stabilizers!"

"Well they're not working very well, are they?"

I take a deep breath.

Center myself. Then slap him. "Get out."

"Gladly."

He grabs his keys and his jacket. The door slams shut.

In the bedroom, I flip open my journal, rereading what I've written, what he's read.

March 5th—*Another pimple on my cheek. I've counted seven. It looks like someone ordered a pizza to my face.*

March 6th—*I unraveled. See? This morning. I came apart like paper in water, I ripped up, I shredded, I want out of this body, I am afraid of this face. I want to tear off these dresses, take them off, I can't be here, I can't be here.*

March 7th—*Life has always been pretty hard farming, and at this point, I kind of just want it to be over.*

March 8th—*Dr. T. upped the Lithium. I don't feel a fucking thing.*

March 9th—*Marcie asked me what it was like to date Ben. I told her it was like adopting a golden retriever.*

March 10th—*He is the puppy, I am the bitch.*

I run hot water in the pale yellow bathtub, peel off my rings and bracelets, unfurl my hair from its clumsily wadded bun. Rising steam fogs the mirror, erasing mascara streaks and swollen eyes. The water scalds my hand, but I step in anyway, no slip flowers on the tub's base sandpapery against my heels. Tight streaks of muscle unclench in my back. I soak. Olivia tried it here, cooking herself before cutting herself. Warm water running to blood. A stretch, a tear. Death like a birth. My toes bob out of the water. Breathe air. The crackle of static softens to snow.

I pull on a tank top and borrow the bottom half of my father's gray sweat suit. He wore it as he bent to peel up sand dollars in the wind, brushing off silt with dry thumbs. The lamp on the piano has a hollow base of glass, filled with coral and sea urchin shells. It illuminates the living room as I kneel to gather my mother's papers, replace them in their box. Take them out to the garage.

Olivia is in there, doing laundry, chewing on a bobby pin. *Takes a lot of bleach to get blood out of blankets.* She kicks the washing machine with her slipper. *Take it from me. When you slit your wrists, stay in the tub.*

I recognize the fabric she's loading—the swatches that make up my bedroom quilt. But instead of scraps, they are blouses and dresses. Whole.

"Listen," I say, setting the box down. "I don't blame you for what you did. But maybe I have a little more self-control."

Oh yes. She takes my chin in her hand. *You're the queen of self-control.*

"That doesn't mean I'll make the same choice."

She studies my face. *I wish you wouldn't wear my costume jewelry like its real jewelry.*

I touch my earrings. "I got these at a craft fair."

It's not a choice.

"Are you saying there's no free will?"

Free will was when I chose between eggs and oatmeal. Lolling her head to the side, she mimes hanging herself. *That wasn't a choice.*

"If it wasn't a choice, it wasn't a sin. And if it wasn't a sin, you should be in heaven. Or, Jesus, I don't know! Purgatory, at least."

You'll have to pass that on to the authorities.

"What are you doing in the garage?"

She looks at me. *This is my heaven. Doing laundry for eternity. Being insulted by my little girl.* She throws her hands in the air. *Hallelujah. Glory be!*

And then she is gone.

Breathing mold spores in the dark, I listen for Ben. My hair is a tangle of wet snakes on the pillow. The radiator cooks dust, humming with heat. Finally: a fumbling at the front door, keys clanking to the counter. Ben runs water in the kitchen, opens the fridge. *The bedroom the bedroom the bedroom*, I will him. *Don't sleep on the couch.*

"Hey," he says. He is standing in the doorway, backlit by the bathroom light.

"Hey." I pat the scratchy comforter.

Steadying himself with the doorframe, bracing one foot against the other in turn, he steps out of his sneakers. He flops on the bed, smelling like paint flecks and deodorant and crushed leaves.

I pick a piece of lint from my sweat pants. "Sorry I smacked you."

"Eh. You're not that strong."

I hold my toes, cold outside the covers. "You shouldn't have read my diary."

"You shouldn't have lied to me."

I point to myself. "Sin of omission." I point to him. "Sin of commission."

"Technicalities. What matters is that we can trust each other."

"I have a lot of baggage."

"Everyone has baggage."

"Mine's heavier."

He rubs my back, trailing his hand between my shoulder blades. "You know, you also wrote about how much you like me."

"Yeah?"

"Yeah. Pages and pages. It was really sweet."

Ben and I look at each other across the pillow. I expect to see something in those dark pools—some secret, some answer. But I just see his eyes, soft and moist. A creature unafraid of scrutiny because he hasn't been hurt.

"You know what the thing about my mom is? The thing that scares me?"

"Huh?"

“I don’t think it was a choice.”

Ben touches my hair. “You always have a choice.”

“I don’t want my story to end like that.”

“It won’t.”

“I’m not sure I believe that.”

“What can I do?”

“To what?”

“To make you believe it?”

I shut my eyes, and doorway light blurs the blackness. Rising from the carpet: the smell of damp towels and broken sand dollars. Ben’s fingers trace the side of my face, fingering my earrings, stroking the tiny wisps of fur along my earlobes.

I blink, a cavern of birds opening in my stomach.

“I don’t know.”

✲ ELEPHANTS NEVER FORGET ✲

FROM: janiceaureliagibbs@honeylocusttech.edu
TO: splunkmiester@splunkspace.com
DATE: Wednesday, April 23, at 10:35PM
SUBJECT: Your Book!!!

Dear Cody,

I was in the bookstore getting bored with my medical terminology flashcards, kicking myself for buying a rip-off $3.00 iced coffee that took 3 seconds to drink, when I saw this guy reading a book titled *Elephants Never Forget.* The cover featured an orange elephant silhouette against an ivory background. I squinted at the author's name: Cody Splunk. I spit my coffee out. I did. I literally *spit* it. I was like, "Dude, my friend wrote that book!" The guy looked at me like I was crazy and pointed to an ENTIRE STACK of *Elephants Never Forget.* Cody! There are, like, 5 copies of your book sitting there, which indicates that people are buying them, and possibly even reading them. That is so cool! You must be, like, rolling around on your bed in a gigantic pile of cash. I've only gotten through the first chapter so far, but I like what you are doing with the futuristic dystopia where exotic wildlife are extinct and people believe that elephants are mystical creatures. I don't know why GovCo, the sinister government-corporation hybrid kidnapped the protagonist's girlfriend, but I'm sure Clint McClintock and his ruggedly handsome face will get to the bottom of the conspiracy. Nice author photo, by the way. Where'd you get the horse?

Update on me: I ditched Texas for the brave new world of Kentucky. Piggott, Kentucky to be precise. What? You haven't heard of Piggott, Kentucky? Don't worry, no one has. It is, however, the jam capital of Kentucky. It also boasts a museum with over 300 wax figures depicting the Old and New Testament. The museum also has two rooms of Christian martyrs, and Kentucky's largest Braille Bible.

I'm living with my Dad and Stepmom, which actually isn't bad. In Texas I had, like, a weekly screaming match with Glenda. Once I threw a cat at her. But now we enjoy secretly smoking cigarettes on the porch. I'm working on my Radiology Tech degree, and I've got a work-study job at the Student Success Center. I must say that I am a fan of the desk job. I pretty much sit here, do my homework, and occasionally tell people to sign the binder. But when I graduate with my degree, I can make up to, like, $52,000 a year! Then it will be me rolling around on a pile of cash! Yahahahaha!

Anyway, my boss is due back from her lunch break, so I should pretend to be working. Write back if you have a minute! I'd love to know what's new with you, Mr. "I-had-a-write-up-in-*The Rio Grande Star*-and-neglected-to-tell-my-old-friend."

Stay cool,
Janice

FROM: splunkmeister@spunkspace.com
TO: janiceaureliagibbs@honeylocusttech.edu
DATE: Thursday, April 24, at 9:32AM
SUBJECT: RE: Your Book!

Dear Janice,

SO GREAT TO HEAR FROM YOU!!! I've been responding to all of this fan mail asking boneheaded questions like, "So how did elephant DNA get written into Clint McClintock's DNA in the first place? And it's like, did you even read past page 300, sir? I waste hours responding to such queries, when I should really be working on my sequel, *Elephants Never Forget II: Elephant Burial Grounds.* Anyway, it was amazing to open the 99th e-mail with the subject line "Your Book!" and find a miracle: Janice Gibbs.

It sounds like you have all your marbles in one sock, as my grandma says. Radiology Tech is a good degree. My sister was thinking about going for that, but instead she decided to go for sitting in front of the TV drinking microwaved ice cream. When my book came out, everyone in the family quit their jobs, so finances are actually kind of tight! Nonetheless, it is amazing to buy the things we've always needed, like Tory's asthma meds and Greebo's Hummer dealership.

I am actually doing a reading in Lexington in May (crazy coincidence!). I looked it up and it's only two and a half hours from Piggott. I can make the drive in my rental car, *no problem*, if you feel like having lunch. I'll have my assistant call you. Kidding! (I don't have an assistant! But sometimes Tory pretends to be my assistant on the phone, and then people are like, "Why does your assistant make those weird growling noises?") Anyways, let me know if you're up for it. It would make my decade!

Your friend,
Cody

FROM: janiceaureliagibbs@honeylocusttech.edu
TO: splunkmeister@splunkspace.com
DATE: Sunday, May 25, at 2:38AM
SUBJECT: blast from the past

Hey Splunkmeister—

When you set off the alarm in the wax museum, I had a flashback to sneaking around *Bridges*. Sigh. Those were the days. Actually, though, they kind of weren't. I'm way happier now. Sorry there was gravel in your burger. Small town—not too many dining options.

It was hard for me to answer your question about why I finally left the Valley. To elaborate: After my brush with the law, I was in this halfway house, eating expired egg salad, getting my underwear stolen. The duffel bag of stuff I scavenged from my aunt's rampage included one reading item: Ms. Freedman's diary. So lying under a moth-eaten blanket, too depressed to move, I took up and read. The stroll down memory lane inspired me to contemplate the awful fates of our homeroom frenemies.

1) Julie Chang: Got a traumatic brain injury in Iraq.

2) Kristi Colimote: Drank a bottle of Lysol to get attention from her boyfriend. When he found her 3 days later, her left side was dead and her kidneys were shot. (He did not stick around to help her with the catheter.)

3) Phil Gasher: Got hit over the head with a tube sock of combination locks at Huntsville State Penitentiary.

And I was like, okay, Ms. Freedman, you failed. Why couldn't you have been the teacher from one of those movies where a nice lady with good bone structure stands on her desk and reads a poem and the kids are all like, fuck poverty, we're going to college!

Lying there under the scratchy blanket, I was feeling how hopeless it is to try to help or save people, because their lives keep going forward like trains on a track, moving toward the gaping maw grinding jaw of evil fate. Then I got to the part of the journal where Ms. Freedman gets batshit crazy/biblical: "*Isaiah 45:9: The clay does not ask the potter: what are you making?*"

Meaning: we are clay, God's taking pottery 101. Meaning: ain't our place asking God why she keeps mashing our faces in. We may think the ashtray is getting ruined, but, surprise! God is really making us into gorgeous Precious Moments figurines.

I find this problematic because for one, Precious Moments are creepy. Two: in this halfway house, the saying "God don't make mistakes" gets bandied about like a favorite beach ball. Sherrie says, "I feel bad that I was a meth-whore and CPS took my eleven kids," and Amber says, "That's okay, Sherrie, God don't make mistakes."

But it wasn't God who made Sherrie the blowjob queen of the I-80 underpass. She did that to herself! Yes, Sherrie got molested by her uncle and abused by her husband and the sciatica made it hard for her to keep that factory job, but God didn't light that first bowl under her then-existent teeth.

I have the same problem with the "The clay does not ask the potter 'what are you making?'" thing. Because, honestly: I do not think God made me into a broke homeless pill-popping thief. Some bad shit happened to me, yes. But God didn't hold a lightning bolt to my head and say: "Janice A. Gibbs, you swallow Shirley's Diazepam. Take a fifty from the cash drawer. Keep fucking up your life so I can make you into a useless ceramic ashtray." Even now, if I wanted to, I could swallow my pride, call Glenda, and say, "Wire me money for a bus ride to Piggot. I'm coming home."

Then I realized: I should just fucking do that.

So I did.

Good luck with the Rags2Riches shoot. I'm sure it will get you a lot of publicity, but it seems like the host chick is all about the drama. She's always trying to reunite "Riches" with, like, childhood bullies from when they were "Rags." I've seen, like, fifteen slap fights on that show. So. Be warned.

Love,
J.

[Transcript of TeenTV's *Rags2Riches*]

(Wide shot of CODY SPLUNK on horseback in JANICE'S front yard. Cut to HARPER.)

HARPER: This Riches is getting ready for his horseback proposal. Cody, are you feeling the butterflies?

CODY: Uh, yeah.

HARPER: I'm ringing the door for you, okay? *(Rings bell.)*

JANICE: *(Opens door.)*

HARPER: I'm Harper, and this is RAGS 2 RICHES.

JANICE: Dear God. *(Clutches forehead.)*

HARPER: Do you remember Cody Splunk?

JANICE: (*irritably*) I had lunch with him last week.

HARPER: He's gone from RAGS . . . to RICHES! *(HARPER steps back.)*

CODY: *(Horse clops into view.)* Janice Gibbs. *(Proffers ring.)* Will you marry me?

JANICE: What?

HARPER: The nerd is getting with the Goth girl, peoples! This is so freaking sweet!

JANICE: Oh my God. Cody. Get off the horse.

HARPER: This was his idea, angel-face.

CODY: *(Looking unsure.)* What sayest thou, my lady Janice? Your white horse awaits ye.

HARPER: That's a forty- carat diamond, girl. I'd put that on if I were you.

JANICE: Listen, shut that off.

HARPER: (*Pointing at Janice.*) My cameras do what they want.

JANICE: I will bite off your finger, so help me God.

HARPER: He's already turned it off. No need to be so sensitive.

JANICE: Cody. What were you thinking?

CODY: That I love you.

JANICE: *(Shaking head.)* You can't.

CODY: But I do.

JANICE: You can't just, have a lunch date and then ask me to marry you a week later. It doesn't work like that.

CODY: *(Closes helmet visor. Spurs horse. Horse trots a few feet, then chews on gladiolas.)*

HARPER: There he goes, peoples! Galloping into the distance!

JANICE: I thought you said that thing was off.

HARPER: Janice, tell the viewers why you shot this Riches down.

JANICE: You are a TERRIBLE PERSON.

HARPER: You're the one who broke his heart, doll.

JANICE: *(Slams door.)*

journal. "Janice," she says, sticking out her hand. "I got two days off work, I can help with the flyers."

"Can you hold her?" you ask the girl, trading baby for journal. Your wife's neat, even, handwriting is on the cover. *Laura's Journal of Mystery and Wonder. McAllen, Texas. August 2004.* "I'm not supposed to read this," you say.

The girl jiggles Rose, humming deep and low. Rose sputters, hiccups. Blinks open her eyes.

You set the journal on the coffee table, go into the kitchen for a drink. Your wife's best friend hands you a glass of amber liquid. You down it. She gives you a hug. "Ben," she says. "This is not your fault." Then she goes back to stacking flyers emblazoned with photos of your wife. *Missing. Reward.* In the pictures she is laughing, wearing lipstick. She looks normal. She looks fine.

At night you push the baby around the neighborhood, the neighborhood your wife thought was perfect. "Downward mobility!" she shouted, laughing too loud. Most people in this neighborhood have only odd jobs, and she liked this. She called it downward mobility, but it was more like playing poor, with family purse strings within easy tugging distance. You pass a yard with five chihuahuas wearing striped, collared shirts. They throw themselves against the chain link fence, barking wildly.

Someone is sleeping in a scratched white Chevy. It is the skeleton girl. Sleeping in her shitty car. You knock on the window. She sits straight up, startled. It takes her a moment to recognize you. She rolls down the window. "Yeah?"

You don't know why you knocked. "Aren't you cold?"

"I'm okay."

"We have an extra bedroom."

She evaluates your face. Shrugs.

Inside, you show her the spare room, into which your wife banished your GameCube, your TV. Corded monsters, she called them. Vampires of the inner life.

"I can take the baby," the girl says. "If you want to get some rest." She flops on the bed, pats her stomach.

You lay the baby on her. Sit down on a rocking chair. "How do you know Laura?"

"I was a feral raccoon who drove her to madness." She watches your reaction. "She was my English teacher."

You rub your eyes.

"I was at the wedding, actually."

The wedding.

Your cheeks grow wet.

"Have you been bargaining?"

"I'm sorry?"

"I've been bargaining. If they find her safe, I have to go to say a rosary every day for the rest of my life."

"I don't believe in God."

"I don't believe in bargaining." She kisses Rose's head. "I always bargain, though."

"I thought she could do it. I thought if she tried harder. If I tried harder."

"Some things you can't do by trying."

"What else is there?"

Janice slowly strokes Rose's head. "You should sleep."

"I can't sleep."

"Then read the journal." Janice uses her right foot to push off her left tennis shoe. "Maybe there's a clue."

I sit there.

"Want to get the light?" Janice says.

"Okay." You stand up. Flip the switch.

"You'll find her, Ben," Janice says into the dark.

In the living room, you pour yourself another. Lay down on sofa. Open your wife's journal. Read.

✯ RESURRECTION SNOW GLOBE ✯

Laura's Journal of Mystery & Wonder

McAllen, Texas ~ August 2004

August 16

Billboards of note on the drive down to McAllen:

"Vaginal Rejuvenation—Experience Love again!"

"Club Fantasy Gentleman's Club, TOTALLY EXPOSED! Girls! Sports! Fried Fish Buffet!"

"Need Directions?—GOD"

My roommates: three volunteers in their second year, already on the verge of escaping to grad school/med school/law school. The house—a dilapidated former convent—has stored volunteers since the program's Texas inception. I dump my stuff in the small yellow room upstairs, jimmy open windows with a butcher knife, smash cockroaches with empty jars. The room bears marks of residents past: a window box of geranium skeletons. Empty prescription bottles in the trash. Downstairs, there is an empty, humid chapel and a weight room with antiquated hand weights, a full-length mirror, and a poster of a muscled Jesus doing a push up with the cross on his back. *Sins of the world,* the poster reads. *Try bench-pressing this.*

Housemates: Araceli, Margo, and Philip. Araceli irons her shirts, gels her hair into a sleek black ponytail, and deals with the stress of teaching science by running ultramarathons.

Margo teaches kindergarten. She has a resigned expression, sadness bitten in at the lip as she hums tunelessly in the kitchen, chopping chard.

Philip teaches middle school music. He wears a short-sleeved button-down printed with small blue birds. He has grey eyes and a prickly half-beard. On his bookshelf, *Franny and Zooey* leans against *Pedagogy of the Oppressed.*

Am instantly in love.

August 17

Vice principal oriented me to Joseph P. Anderson. Ms. Campos is a sinewy, spiky-haired white lady with an irritated face. She has Texas Longhorns regalia all over her office. She wears beige pantsuits and high heels, and walks around barking into a walkie-talkie.

She scares the shit out of me.

August 18

School mascot: The Anaconda. Large posters line the hallways. "Anacondas are Achievers." A laminated newspaper article is stuck to the wall above the drinking fountain: *Students Need Less Coddling, More Rules and Tasks, Experts Say*. Two girls stare grimly out of the picture, clutching brooms.

There are these metal cage-things that come down and block the halls if there are riots.

Mentor teacher in classroom next door is Mr. Kopecky, a tall, silver-haired man. Came by classroom to give a pep talk. Told story about first job: when nine, he sold pink popcorn at a freak show. One of the freaks was "dogboy," a mute and deformed young man. "I shoved pink popcorn through the bars of his cage," Mr. Kopecky said. "I got fired for feeding pink popcorn to the dog boy."

Not sure how this relates to teaching.

August 19

Eight hours laminating construction paper bear nametags. Because that is what will win them over. Construction paper bears.

August 20

Two hours selecting teacherly outfit. Went with long gray skirt, teal cardigan, and glasses.

I leaned in Philip's doorway. He was sitting in bed, annotating rosters.

"Do I look like a teacher?"
He threw back his head and laughed.
"What?"
"My God. You look like a librarian."
"Why do I feel like I should have a puff paint sweater with addition and subtraction on it? And a denim smock?"
"You're thinking elementary school."
"I feel like an imposter."
"Fake it 'till you make it."
"And here I thought I was supposed to seek authentic selfhood."
"No." Philip said. "Better to be a simulacrum of society's organized despair."

August 22

Mass at Our Lady of Sorrows. While the church is 90% Hispanic, it has a life size Aryan Jesus mannequin hanging from the cross above the altar. The deacon gave a homily about two undocumented immigrants who came to his door, seeking water. He convinced them to turn themselves in to the border patrol.

Dear God!

August 23

"Family dinner" night. Philip made balsamic roasted butternut squash with hot chilies and honey.

On my night, I served Raisin Bran.

August 24

First day of school.

Me: Welcome to English 3. Let's play a game to learn each other's names.
Phil Gasher: We should play boner tag.
Me: That is inappropriate language for the classroom.
Janice Gibbs: Plus boner tag is totally gay.
Me: That is *also* inappropriate language.
Julie Chang: But it's not wrong to be gay, miss. Lots of people are gay.
Danny Ramirez: *(to Julie)* Yeah, like you.
Me: OKAY. We do not use the word *gay* as an insult in this classroom. Using

the word gay as an insult perpetuates a negative stereotype. And if you need to say something, you RAISE YOUR HAND.

Kristi Colimote: *(raises hand)*

Me: Kristi?

Kristi Colimote: It's ʻcuz on TV, I saw these two chicks getting married and one of them was with short hair and dressed like a dude.

Amelia Basil: *(under breath)* Sodomites!

Me: OKAY. Everyone, grab a pen or pencil from your backpack, and take a look at the worksheet on your desk.

Janice Gibbs: But what about the game, Miss?

Danny Ramirez: Boner tag?

Me: Danny, you just got an hour in ISS.

Danny Ramirez: You laughed when Phil Gasher said it!

Janice Gibbs: Yeah, miss, he can't get in trouble if you laugh.

Me: *(Filling out form.)* Here. You go to ISS. Now.

Danny Ramirez: (*leaving*) You hate me because I'm black!

For the record: Danny is Latino.

August 26

I offered them *A Wrinkle in Time* or *Catcher in the Rye*. I gave a dramatic reading of the first page of each.

"Those books are boring, Miss."

"We should read *Pirates of the Caribbean*."

"I believe that is a movie."

"Nuh-uh Miss. It's even on the shelf."

And indeed. The novelized version of the *Pirates of the Caribbean* film was on the shelf.

"That's not really literature," I said.

August 27

"So I'm reading them a book," I told Philip, "Which was based on a movie. Which was based on a *ride at Disneyland*."

Philip jabbed fork-holes in a yam with assured, graceful stabs. "At least they're listening to you read."

"I mean, if it were the other way around, it would be okay. If there was a Disneyland ride based on *The Catcher in the Rye*, that would be sweet."

Philip picked up my side ponytail and placed it behind my shoulder. I stared at him, touched by the intimate gesture. Disoriented.

"Your hair was in your tea."

I set my mug on the counter. "So it was."

August 31

After school, Ms. Campos came by to yell at me for not being at the curriculum meeting.

"I didn't know there was a curriculum meeting."

"There was a memo in your box."

"I didn't know I had a box."

"C'mon," she said, jerking her head towards the hallway. She led me to a meeting room filled with ELA instructors. "Ms. Freedman wasn't aware there was a curriculum meeting," Ms. Campos said. "Please get her up to speed."

Turns out: I am supposed to be working through a state-issued mass-produced reader, drilling kids on fused sentences and comma splices. While Mr. Kopecky went through slides, I skimmed the reader. After three sentences I wanted to gouge out my eyes.

September 1

"Aw miss, this is boring."

"Why do we have to do this stupid worksheet?"

"We wanna to keep reading our book."

"We wanna write in our journals, miss."

"I don't understand," I said. "When I was reading *Pirates* last week, Danny stuck a fork in the light socket. During journal time last week, Janice tried to light Kristi's hair on fire."

The students looked at me blankly.

"Let's make a deal. As soon as you finish your worksheet, I'll read another chapter."

Worksheets became projectiles. Worksheets became face blotters, spit wads, origami doves, dirty notes on the floor.

"Have it your way," I said. "No *Pirates*. Just more worksheets tomorrow."

"Then we'll just ditch the class, miss."

"Then you'll just get detention, Danny."

"Don't be a hater, miss."

"Don't ditch class, Danny."

"You hate me because I'm black!"

"That doesn't even make any sense," I said. "Class dismissed."

September 2

"What's the point of being a teacher if I'm just supervising rote memorization and worksheet completion?" I said to Philip. "A robot could do that."

He looked up from his grapefruit. "And when they develop the technology to build that robot," he said, "you'll be out of a job."

September 3

Janice Gibbs: a feral child with excessive eye shadow and stringy black hair that obscures her face. I feel a daily urge to take scissors to it. She has an anti-authoritarian complex that would be interesting were it not so ill informed.

During lunch period today, she perched on a desk next to mine.

"What's that you're eating there, miss?

"Rice and beans."

"Gross."

"I acknowledge it's a little bland. I overcompensate with salt."

"That's gonna make you bloat, Miss."

"It's a risk I'm willing to take. What's for lunch in the cafeteria?"

"Fish sticks. I threw it out."

"What? Fish sticks are fun! You can dip them in ketchup."

"I never eat lunch. I don't eat breakfast either."

"You know that's terrible for you, right?"

"I'm not hungry in the morning. After school I go to Circle K and get Hot Cheetos, a pickle and a Coke."

"Dear God." I handed her my apple. "Please eat this. You're probably about to get scurvy."

"Like the pirates?" she asked, biting into the apple.

"Exactly."

September 6

"Lockdown," Mrs. Gutierrez announced over the intercom this morning. I locked the door, cut the lights, ordered students to get under their desks. Ms.

Campos came by and shook the door handle. It opened. She stepped into the room. "Bang. Bang. Bang," she said, pointing her finger at me. "You're dead."

September 7

Called into Mrs. Gutierrez's office to be redressed for lockdown failure.

Mrs. Gutierrez: All your students are dead.
Me: If it had been a real attack. Yes.
Mrs. Gutierrez: How do you feel about that, Ms. Freedman?
Me: Relieved.
Mrs. Gutierrez: I'm sorry?
Me: Relieved it wasn't a real lockdown!

Mrs. Gutierrez sent me home with a binder on lockdown procedure. Apparently, when a perturbed gunman (or rather, gunchild) bursts into the classroom, the worst thing to do is remain calm. The class should pelt him with a rain of textbooks and pencils. The four burliest students should tackle and disarm him.

Will remember this next time Campos busts in.

September 8

Snooped in Philip's room. A picture of his girlfriend (Tessa) rests on his windowsill in a clear plastic frame. She has russet hair and excellent cheekbones. I turned the picture over.

I don't have to say it, she has written. *You already know.*

What a fucking bitch.

September 9

Lithium side effect: subcutaneous pimples, hard nutty globes of pain. Makes me feel like a decaying leper who should stay in her leper cave, or at least wear a veil in social situations.

Small pink pills, sticking in my throat.

September 10

I strolled through the downtown strip, passing clubwear outlets, taco stands, shops selling bright silk flowers, dollar stores cluttered with quick-dying batteries, blank baseball caps, and nail clippers emblazoned with the Virgin Mary. Girls wearing hoop earrings sat on hot black benches, gentle rolls of belly fat sticking out from midriff tops. Pregnant mothers rolled strollers down Main Street, their kids forking cheese smeared Hot Cheetos from foil bags. Old men in cowboy hats congregated on the corners, thumbs tucked in belt buckles, eyes following legs.

As I walked back to the convent, I saw a woman leaning against the back wall of the rectory, holding the sides of her skirt. Then I noticed the stream of liquid splattering between her legs. "Estoy urinando," she said imploringly. "No hay baños en esas tiendas."

I am peeing. There are no bathrooms in these stores.

September 12

Kristi Colimote, on her boyfriend: My cousin was all, "Do you love him?" And I was like, "Yes." She was like, "If you love him, you'll drink this jar of pickle juice." So I drank it. Then I threw up.

September 13

After dinner, Philip and I sit on the porch, chewing on mesquite pods.

"Do you love your girlfriend?"

"Yes."

"If you love her, you'll drink a jar of pickle juice."

"I don't follow your logic."

"So you're not going to drink it?"

"No. That's disgusting."

"That's what I thought."

September 14

Margo and Araceli invited me to go to South Padre Island Friday night. South Padre is a famous party beach—the kind of place where MTV does its Spring Break show, the kind of place where "Girls Gone Wild" gets filmed. For two weeks in April, it's packed with bikini-clad flashers and intoxicated frat boys. The rest of the year, it's a typical tourist destination—bars, hotels, restaurants. Palm trees, warm water. Fine white sand. Two hours from the poorest county in the nation, you can sip a seven-dollar margarita at the beachfront bar, and watch the sun bob messily into the waves.

After a two-hour drive, we got gelato in cones, walked down to the water. Except for a few late night strollers, the beach was abandoned. Araceli mashed the last of her gelato into her mouth, and made a beeline for the waves. She jumped in, splashing in swirling whitewater up to her shins. "It's warm!" she shouted, the wind whipping her hair around her face. I slipped off my flip-flops. The water buzzed, a warm cola at my feet.

"It's like a bath." Margo stood in the water up to her ankles, jeans rolled just below her knees.

I was used to the prickle of the Pacific. An ocean that turned arms to cold rubber, spat me back hollow, chilled. This water was like the womb. A nurturing broth. A place for pink, undeveloped souls to bob before they're born. I watched saltwater dampen the strings of my jean skirt, tangle them in foam. The moon was a bright shard. I stepped deeper into the water, soaking my skirt. The water was dark like liquor. When I slapped at foam, phosphorescent algae sparked with glints of fiery light.

September 15

I imagine myself sticking my hand into my ribcage, pulling out shards of colored glass, waving them under Philip's nose. "See, see?" I ask, shaking them slightly. "Do you see what's inside of me?"

I finally broke down and put the air conditioning on. I am imagining that this kills thousands of baby seal pups.

It would be nice if Philip were here to enjoy this air conditioning with me. Imagine: Instead of touching my arm and saying, "God, you're sweaty," he could say: "All of that colored glass you keep pulling out of your ribs would make a nice window, maybe in a church."

September 16

Janice hung around my desk again at lunch.

"What'd you do this weekend, miss?"

"My housemates and I went to South Padre Island."

"I love South Padre! I went there for Mardi Gras last year. I was in the back of the truck and this other truck of guys has some beads and I'm all, 'give me some,' and they throw one and then they're like, 'Now you have to show us something.' And I'm like, 'You're not seeing any of this, this, or *this*.' And they're like, 'You owe us!' And I'm like, 'The only thing you're seeing is *this*.'" She flips up her middle finger.

September 17

Bush leading by four percent. Let us sit down on the curb of the pavement and weep.

September 18

"You know what I had to scrub off a desk today?" I told Señora Gomez in the copy room. "ROBERTO RUIZ SUCKS BLACK COCK."

Señora Gomez sipped her coffee. "Sounds like Roberto is making some poor life choices."

I stood there for a moment, holding my files. "Your comment could be interpreted as both racist and homophobic."

"*Mija*," Senora Gomez said. "A 14-year old should not be sucking cock of any race, creed, color, or nationality."

"What's the age cut off?"

"How do you mean?"

"At what point is cock-sucking acceptable? 16? 18?"

"Ms. Freedman, this is sexual harassment in the workplace," Señora Gomez said, and walked out.

September 22

Conversation Between me and God:

Me: Hi. What's up?

God: Silence.

Me: So. I feel like I always end up talking about myself. Let's talk about you for a change.

God: Silence.

Me: What's on your mind?

God: My children and how they suffer.

Me: Oh. Right. I'll get on that.

September 28

In a punishing mood, I put on a baseball hat and earphones and an inch thick coat of sunscreen and went running on the track along the canal. I cranked the volume on my cd player, playing slit-your-wrists indie dissonance, sun glinting bright on my damp face, the exhaust from cars like the warm breath of lambs.

September 29

A low moan in my bones: I want to go home I want to go home.

October 1

Leaving campus at six P.M., saw Campos yanking kid (I am assuming her own) by the shirt into her car. He had a square of masking tape over his mouth.

October 2

Seven is God's perfect number, Amelia Basil informed me today. Who knew?

October 3

Janice Gibbs, on family: "Once, my dad's girlfriend pulled my hair. So I threw a cat at her. It landed on her back, and she was crying."

October 5

Painted in dust on the back of a van: *I wish my wife was this dirty.*

Message painted below it, in a different hand: *She is.*

October 6

Momentum trickling out like someone poked a hole in my foot. Lithium, I am going to flush you down the toilet.

October 7

Kristi, on family: "My dad is nothing to me. I've never met him. When I was in my mom's stomach he locked her in a room for two days with no food or water for lying to him. He asked her if she smoked his last cigarette, and she said no. After he let her out, she beat him up and left."

October 8

Cooked dinner. Garlic stinging under my fingernails. Hold it together, damn it. Hold it together.

October 10

Philip and I shared a pint of Ben & Jerry's and watched a special on a man with a face-eating tumor. It was followed up by a special about a resilient woman with no legs. She worked a job, married, and reared a baby. Legless. With a terrific attitude. She made me feel like shit.

October 11

Kristi, on neighbors: Our neighbors are Filipino and I hate them. Yesterday their dog got out and it started attacking our dog. "Why don't you go back to your own country," I said, "if you can't even take care of your dog?"

"I'll kill your dog," the man said.

"I'll kill you," I said. Then I started punching him and my mom had to tear me away so he didn't press charges. Then she gave me a beer to calm down, 'cuz when I start to fight people they press charges. So I just drank a bottle and then we went and had fun.

October 12

Bought sandwich cookies for parent teacher conference, set them out on flimsy paper plates.

Phil Gasher's Dad: *(Looking me over.)* I have concert T-shirts older than you.
Me: And I bet they're equally effective at classroom management.
Mr. Gasher: *(Blank look of confusion.)*
Me: Never mind.

October 13

Kristi and her posse populated my doorway after school.

Kristi: Have you heard the rumor?
Me: What rumor?
Kristi: People are saying that I'm pregnant.

Me: Are you?
Kristi: No.
Me: Um, well. Congratulations, then, I guess.

October 14

Andy Lopez: Miss? There's something I've been meaning to tell you.
Me: Yes?
Andy Lopez: Last week, I saw a dead rat.
Me: Okay.
Andy Lopez: Ants were coming out of its eyes.
Me: Thanks for letting me know.

October 15

First line in Phil Gasher's essay: *Saving lives is so amazing it will put a dent in your heart.*

October 16

Character Flaws:

*Fear that dogs will see into my soul and growl at me.
*Fear that babies will see into my soul and cry when I hold them.
*Fear, basically, that something is rotten at my core, and that people will see through to my rotten, shameful, center.

October 17

In college, Lakshmi's mother took us out to tea, and gently stroked my ear. "You have lucky earlobes," she said. She gazed at my collarbone. "But those moles around your neck could be a noose."

I thought of myself at 17, making a noose from an extension cord in the garage. My mother, swinging from a rafter. Why the garage, with these dark moments? Why always the garage?

October 18

Kristi stayed in the classroom during lunch, drawing on the back of a comma-splice worksheet.

"What's up, Kristi?"

"I'm pregnant."

I sat down beside her. "How are you feeling?"

"Bad. But kind of good, also. I don't know."

"Yeah?"

"I think I know what I'm gonna name it."

"Yeah?"

"Savannah."

She indicated her doodle.

Printed on it, in large block letters: SUFANA.

October 19

After dinner, Philip leaned into my doorway. "I have a present for you."

"What's the occasion?"

"Your first pregnant student!" He handed me a small plastic toy. "Think of it as a consolation prize. I found it in the Korean discount store."

It was a plastic snow globe depicting Christ's resurrection. Half the glitter water had leaked out. Christ was wading in it waist-deep, arms raised before his tomb. Bowing, golden-haired angels flanked him. When I shook it, the water frothed a little, the glitter spun. Plastic Jesus, drowning in a whirlpool bubble bath. A resurrection snow globe.

"You're trying to cheer me up with a tchotchke?"

Philip flopped on my bed. "I thought it was funny."

I turned it over, and squinted to read the tiny print. "*Made in Hong Kong.* God. This was probably made in a sweatshop."

"Yup."

I shook the snow globe. "And Jesus wept."

"Yeah, well. Merry Christmas."

October 20

Have not yet been able to heal and transform any kid in the deep and powerful way they needed to be healed and transformed.

Get on it, teacher-face.

October 21

When I walked outside to bring an empty milk jug to the recycling bin, I saw a ghost leaning over the dumpster, eating my thrown-away stew.

No. It was a homeless man. I slipped the milk carton into the trash. "Excuse me," I said. He grinned at me, teeth glinting in the moonlight.

October 22

I woke up covered in aches, wanting a full body massage. I realized I had no one who I could ask for one. And I felt so lonely I wanted to die.

October 30

Me: What are you going to be for Halloween?
Kristi: We're going as babies.
Me: Cute!
Angelica: I mean, that's what we're going as at school.
Kristi: At night we're going to be cheerleaders. We got knee-high boots.
Angelica: We're going to be hooker cheerleaders.
Kristi: *Dead* hooker cheerleaders.
Me: *(Pause.)* That seems inappropriate.

November 1

Two at a time, I climbed the stairs. My body felt itchy and achy. There was ringing in my ears. I ran the tub full of scalding water. If I cooked myself thoroughly, I could climb out of the tub unbroken. Whole.

After forty-five minutes, Philip knocked on the door. "Can I grab my toothbrush?"

"I don't care."

He opened the door. "Jesus, Laura, I thought you had the curtain pulled."

"These bubbles are protecting my modesty."

"Are you okay?"

"You're stressing me out with your invasive questions. Hand me my towel." I caught the ragged pink terrycloth, and stood up, wrapping it around myself.

"What's the matter?"

"All the shoes I like best are made for eight-year-old girls." I stood there, dripping.

He looked at me, bemused. "Yeah. Well. Tess and I broke up."

"We should take a walk."

November 2

I stumbled through my day like a drunken dreamer, flashes of the night lapping over my eyes—wavering weeds, sweet grass, warmth of skin on skin eclipsing the heat of an electric blanket. All day he was like a ghost on my skin. When I showered, I was sorry beads of water washed away his sweat.

November 5

I lie awake, watching his body. His body, like a moonscape in the darkness.

November 8

Not sleeping. I don't want to sleep. I want to crack open the cage of my ribs, scoop out my heart with an ice cream scooper, and stamp it on paper. So he can see: his name is written there. In blood! Ha ha! "Here, look!" I will say. And he will tape it to the fridge.

November 9

That fire inside me sprouting—my mind tingles, clicking at a hundred miles a minute. NOW I can speak to the children without fear. NOW I know what to say. Before I was dormant, a pile of ashes. Now, I'M ON FIRE.

November 12

I must wear pants/ When I go out/ Or they will shake their heads/ And shout: "Hey! Where are her pants?!"

November 18

Ordered leather-bound journals for all the kids. YES. Everyone deserves nice things, for once!!!

November 20

Idea: Jeopardy vocab game. ("VOCAB STAB!") Cardboard from dumpster! Industrial grade glitter glue!

November 22

Ordered 20 pounds of candy hearts custom printed to read: ENGLISH ROCKS! Because ENGLISH ROCKS!

November 23

Thanksgiving break. Philip in California w. fam. Kind of empty. Blank, dull, broken house.

November 24

Optimal life choice: not get out of bed. Ever. Until Philip comes back.

November 25

Philip called. Got back together with his girlfriend, apparently. Over break.

November 30

Stayed home again. Invisible ocean smacking me with waves.

December 1

My heart feels rubbed raw and tender, pulverized and soaked in vinegar.

December 2

There is a world of pain inside me. A profound terrain of hurt.

December 3

My birthday tomorrow. Amazing timing. Happy 23rd birthday, Laura Freedman. Once more you have failed at the most basic and human of tasks: maintaining a romantic relationship for over two weeks.

Jesus, help me to rally. Help me to wallow out of this sorrow. Cupcakes. I will make cupcakes for the class.

December 4

Cupcakes = bad call.

December 5

They are deviant trolls. Feral raccoons devoid of impulse control.

December 6

Why did I think I could do this? Why did I ever think I could do this?

December 7

There is pride in expecting too much from my stunted heart.

December 8

A dingy loudness. Rustling like the wings of sparrows. I keep turning around, thinking I hear creatures running behind me.

December 9

Isaiah 45:9 "The clay does not ask the potter: what are you making?"
Good Lord. Good Lord. What are you making?

December 11

Hurricane warnings went out over the radio this morning—the tail end of Mitch might slam us in its sweep over Northern Mexico. Shops laid sandbags on their stoops, and some merchants are nailing boards over windows. For now, though, the sky is hazy blue. A block from the convent, a truck pulls up to the curb, and a man beckons me to his car through the glinting screen.

December 12

Couldn't sleep. Went outside, lay down in the itchy, squelchy grass, listened to cicadas humming, watched low smears of pink clouds racing across a blue-black sky. The air smelled like taco stand and jasmine flowers. Tinkly music and rowdy yelling wavered over from the cantinas, and some kind of nocturnal birds were squalling from telephone wires or palm trees. The air was thickening in humidity, sign of a coming storm.

December 13

I lie on faded floral sheets, listen to rain lash against the window. The Rio Grande Valley isn't really a valley. It's an alluvial floodplain. When rain comes fast, the dry ground can't soak it up. Floods flash fast. It's devastating to the families in the *colonias* outside town, where electricity is rickety, water running scarce, where families of twelve share one trailer or tin-roofed hut.

I unhook the lock on the balcony screen door, step out into the wind. Hurricane-force gales whip the spindly palm trees on Main Street, thrashing their fronds, bending them back like slingshots. The sky is the shade of ash, smearing itself around unhappily. Thunder tears from its bolted chamber; sound waves ripple through the grass. The rain falls in torrents, in sheets. The temperature drops to frigid. My skirt and shirt plaster to my skin. Lightning streams and crackles: rough yellow, electric pink.

Below: abandoned streets. Rain surging down the gutters, sluicing into drains. Pouring now with fury and intention, dripping from eaves, hurling itself, gathering in angry pools along the sidewalks, filling the drains faster than they suck it down. The pale blue canals, I imagine, chortle brown. They soon will crumble, overflow, spill through.

I stand there with my hands on the balcony railing, fingers freezing white, toes going numb. I stand there. And I watch the waters rise.

✯ LIKE THE RUSSIAN SAID ✯

My sanitary pad heavy with blood, I stumble through the Public Cemetery of Plano. That baby gutted me. Two weeks, still bleeding. Still bloated in body, foggy of mind.

Olivia's grave is easy to find, as she is sitting on it.

"Laura." She drags on her cigarette. "Sit."

I ease down on the grave across from her. "They switched her at the hospital."

"Who, now, hon?"

I rub my scalp. "No one believes me."

"But you have such an honest face."

I cover my face with my hands.

"I warned you."

"I didn't believe you." I wipe my nose. "You can't trust ghosts."

"Oh no?"

"Like in *Hamlet*."

"I never got the chance to read much Shakespeare." She drains a ghostly can of Diet Rite, tosses it behind a bush.

"Hamlet's dad appears to him and says he was murdered by Hamlet's uncle. *Horrible, most horrible. Murder most foul.* Hamlet doesn't know whether to trust him."

"If you can't trust family, who can you trust?"

"That's the thing. The ghost might not be his father. It could be a demon, tempting him to mortal sin."

"I have signed no contract with the fallen one." She raises her left hand. "I do solemnly swear." She stands up. "Now which way do you want it?"

"What?"

She gives me a levelheaded stare.

"I'm not going to do what you did."

"Of course not. You don't have the spine. You'll do pills. Or gas."

"I don't have pills."

"Well, you've got a car, dear. You just need a garage. Or a hose."

I sift damp gravel through my fingers.

"Listen, the house is still empty. They haven't managed to sell it yet. You still have the key, right? It's waiting for you. Get back in the car, drive the five blocks, bam."

"Did you even want these?" I thrust out the roses.

She smells them. "A beautiful bouquet." She tucks it under her arm. "You're a thoughtful girl." She jerks her head to the side. "C'mon."

"I'll ruin Ben's life."

"Honey." She strokes my cheek. "You already did."

Ice cold globes of grapefruit in my chest.

" Stephen."

"Your brother won't mind. If you've lost a mother, you can lose a sister. Didn't a poet say that? '*The art of losing isn't hard to master*'?"

"That's not what she meant."

"Well. You're the one with the degree."

I lean against the hot metal of the car. "This is the worst thing you can do. The worst thing you can do to anyone."

"Believe me, you're doing that kid a favor. You want to end up drowning her in a bathtub?" Olivia wraps her arm around my waist. "Better yet, why don't you wait four years? Be a *good* mommy. Bake cookies with silver sprinkles. Paint a mural on her wall. Be that kid's best friend. Then have your ugly breakdown. Let her pound on the door while you cut at your wrists. Let her think she can *save* you."

I lay my hands over my still-pouchy stomach.

Olivia smoothes my hair. "You're the gun on the mantle, hon. Like the Russian said: You're going to go off."

It's just what happens next.

The garage is blisteringly hot. By the time I get the door closed, I am drenched in sweat. My thighs stick to the seat. I roll down the windows. Blast the air conditioning.

"Stop smoking."

"What does it matter now?"

I am starting to feel it: smog. Sweet oncoming sleep. But a minnow fights the current, pulling with unease.

"Where do I go?"

"Same place I went."

"You're *here*."

"No, no, honey, I'm in heaven. This is just—what do you call it—a temporal projection. A day trip. I'm here to give you safe passage. Ferry you across the Jordan." She unties the bouquet, weaving flower through stem, making a wreath, a crown. She sets it on my head. "I'm your ministering angel."

I stare at her woozily. "I think you're the devil."

She opens her pocketbook. Dabs her forehead with a pink cloth with scalloped edges. Sighs. "What does it matter now?"

"Get thee hence, Satan."

And she is gone.